Cato.

A modernized version of
Joseph Addison's 'Cato, a Tragedy'
in a Three Act Format

Stew Hanley

Contents

Acknowledgment

A very special thank you to Joseph Addison for all his contributions to the world. Although, an Englishman by birth, he was truly a "great American."

Cast of Characters

PORTIUS: Male, late 20's, Cato's son. In love with Lucius's daughter, Lucia.

MARCUS: Male, mid 20's, Cato's son. In love with Lucius's daughter, Lucia.

SEMPRONIUS: Male, 40's, Senator, Enemy of Cato. Loud, boisterous type.

SYPHAX: Male, 60's, General of Numidians, Enemy of Cato. Has white hair.

JUBA: Male, Late 30's, Ally of Cato. In love with Cato's daughter Marcia.

MARCIA: Female, mid 20's, Cato's daughter. Sterner, more serious than Lucia.

LUCIA: Female, early 20's, Lucius's daughter, Meeker than Marcia.

LUCIUS: Male, mid 40's, Senator, Ally of Cato.

CATO: Male, mid 40's, Enemy of Julius Caesar, Father of Portius, Marcus and Marcia.

SENATE MEMBER #1 - #3:   Males, mid 40's, Ally of Cato.

DECIUS: Male, mid 50's, Roman knight, former friend of Cato, now part of Caesar's military.

MUTINY LEADER: Late 20's, soldier type, Enemy of Cato.

SOLDIER #1 - #3:   Males, late 20's, soldier type, Enemy of Cato.

GUARD: Male, late 20's, soldier type, Enemy of Cato.

Synopsis

The action of the play involves the forces of Cato
at Utica, located in the kingdom of Numidia (current
day Tunisia/Algeria region of Northern Africa). Cato, a
Roman Statesman and follower of the Stoic philosophy,
was on the losing side of a civil war against Julius Caesar.
Cato sees Caesar as an enemy of the Roman Republic's
history of liberty, virtue, and other great traditions; a
cruel dictator in short. After the war, Cato and Scipio,
a like-minded Roman general, move their forces to
Numidia; Cato to Utica and Scipio to Thapsus, a couple
days travel away.

Julius Caesar, along with his vast army, have now come
to Northern Africa looking for vengeance. Caesar has
already defeated Scipio and is advancing towards Cato's
position. There Cato awaits his arrival, for a battle that
Cato is most certainly going to lose. Cato has to decide
- fight to the end? surrender? take his own life and save
his family and friends?

Through these events the play deals with larger issues like liberty versus tyranny, and virtue versus corruption. Cato must decide to stand for what he believes in the face of death.

Cato is without much hope, but not alone. He does have Juba, the prince of Numidia and Lucius, a senatorial ally by his side. However, Sempronius, another senator, and Syphax, general of the Numidians, are secretly conspiring against Cato, hoping to draw off the Numidian army from supporting him. Also with Cato are his sons, Portius and Marcus, and daughter, Marcia.

There are a number of love elements to the story. Portius and Marcus, are in love with Lucia, the daughter of Lucius. Juba loves Cato's daughter Marcia, who is also loved by Sempronius. They are all eager to express their love, but given the gravity of the situation they are in, none seem willing to indulge. It is a challenging situation for even a rigid, Stoic as Cato.

ACT I, Scene 1

Setting: A large open hall in the Governor's Palace of Utica.

Cast: PORTIUS, MARCUS

At Rise: PORTIUS is standing, looking out of a window/outside while MARCUS is busy working at a table nearby.

***

PORTIUS

Marcus, the dawn is heavy with clouds, like the fate of Cato and of Rome. Our father's death would take all the guilt of this war away, and close the scene of blood. Already Caesar has ravaged more than half the globe; mankind has grown thin by his sword. Should he go farther, numbers would be wanting to form new battles to support his crimes.

(PORTIUS looks up towards the sky)
What havoc ambition makes among your works!

MARCUS

Your steady temper, Portius, let's you look on rebellion and Caesar in the calm lights of philosophy. But I'm tortured, even to madness, when I think of the proud victor every time he's named. I see that tyrant prancing over fields strewn with Rome's citizens. His horse's hoofs wet with patrician blood! Oh Portius, is there not some uncommon wrath to blast a man who owes his greatness to his country's ruin?

PORTIUS

Believe me, Marcus, it is a wicked greatness, mixed with too much horror to be envied. How can the flame of our father's actions break through the dark cloud of ills that cover him and burn with a more triumphant brightness? He fights for honor, liberty, and for Rome. His sword has only ever fallen on guilty heads. Oppression and tyranny draw all the vengeance of his arm upon them.

MARCUS

What can Cato do against a degenerate world that bows to Caesar? Being trapped here in Utica he's a poor sight of Roman greatness; guarded by Numidians, commanding a feeble army, with an empty senate.

They're all remnants of mighty battles fought in vain.
By the heavens, such things distract my very soul.
Our father's fortune almost tempts me to renounce his
precepts.

PORTIUS

Remember what our father often told us – "the ways
of heaven are dark and intricate, puzzled in mazes, and
confused with errors. We try to understand them in vain,
lost in a fruitless search."

MARCUS

These are suggestions of a mind at ease. Oh Portius, if
you could only know half the griefs that wring my soul,
you wouldn't talk so calmly. Passion unpitied and failed
love have driven daggers in my heart, and aggravate my
other griefs. If only my Lucia were kind!

PORTIUS
(aside, speaking to himself)
Marcus, you do not see that your brother is your rival. But
I must hide it, for I know your temper.

(turns back to speak to MARCUS)
My brother, your virtue is to be proven. Put forth your
utmost strength, work every nerve, and call up our father
in your soul to crush the tyrant love, and guard your heart
from this weakness. That would be a conquest worthy of
Cato's son.

MARCUS

Portius, that advice I cannot take. Instead of healing, it would increase my weakness. For my honor, let me plunge into a war with my worst foes to a certain death. Then you will see that I am not slow to follow glory and confess my father. Love is not to be reasoned down. It is a second life, it grows in the soul, warms every vein, and beats in every pulse. I feel it, but my resolution melts.

PORTIUS

You should behold young Juba, the Numidian prince! You would see how carefully he forms himself to glory, and breaks the fierceness of his native temper to copy our father's bright example. Do you not know he loves our sister Marcia? His eyes, his looks, his actions all betray it. But no matter how it swells within him, his sense of honor drives it back into his heart. Shall an African reproach the great Cato's son, and show a virtue lacking in a Roman soul?

MARCUS

Portius, no more! Whenever did Juba, or yourself, show a virtue that has cast me at a distance, and thrown me out in the pursuits of honor?

PORTIUS

Marcus, I know your temper well. Just the mere appearance of dishonor strikes a fire in you.

MARCUS

A brother's sufferings claim a brother's pity.

PORTIUS

Heaven knows I pity you; look at my eyes. Even while I speak they swim in tears. If you could see my heart, you would see it bleed on your behalf.

MARCUS

Then why do you treat me with rebukes and not kindness?

PORTIUS

Marcus, if I knew how to ease your troubled heart, believe me, I would die to do it.

MARCUS

My brother, my friend! Pardon a weak soul that swells and sinks; it is the sport of passions.

(suddenly MARCUS sees SEMPRONIUS approaching and becomes uneasy)

But wait Sempronius comes. He must not find this softness hanging on me. I must go now.

(MARCUS exits)

ACT I, Scene 2

Setting: A large open hall in the Governor's Palace of Utica

Cast: SEMPRONIUS, PORTIUS

At Rise: PORTIUS now standing over the table, when SEMPRONIUS enters.

***

SEMPRONIUS
(aside, by himself)
Conspiracies should be executed as soon as they are formed! Wait, why is Portius here? I don't like that cold youth. I must speak a language foreign to my heart now.

(walks over to PORTIUS)
Good morning Portius! Let us embrace while we are both

free men! Today's sunrise might be the last to ever rise on Roman liberty.

PORTIUS

Yes, this morning my father called together his little Roman senate to ask them if he can oppose the mighty torrent that bears down on Rome, and all her gods, or should he give up the world to Caesar.

SEMPRONIUS

Not all the pomp and majesty of Rome can raise her senate more than Cato's presence! Oh my Portius, I wish that I could call that wondrous man my father. If only your sister, Marcia, were favorable to my vows, I would be blessed indeed!

PORTIUS

Sempronius! You talk of love to Marcia while her father's life is in danger? You might as well court her as she watched the whole world burn in flames!

SEMPRONIUS

The more I see your wonders, the more I'm charmed. You should take heed, my Portius! The world has all its eyes on Cato's son. Your father's merit sets you up for all to view, and shows you in the fairest of lights to make your virtues, or your faults, obvious.

PORTIUS

Why am I lingering here at this important hour? My

father is debating the events of war; I should be out lifting up the courage of the soldiers with the love of freedom, and contempt of life! I'll thunder their country's cause in their ears, and try to rouse up all that's Roman in them. It's not in mortals to command success, but we'll do more, Sempronius, we'll deserve it.

(PORTIUS exits)

SEMPRONIUS
(by himself now)
Curses on Portius! How he mimics his father! So pompous and ambitious!

(pauses for a few seconds)
But I wonder why old Syphax is not here. His Numidian genius is well-disposed to mischief. Cato has used me, he refused his daughter to my ardent vows. His ruined cause is a bar to my ambition. Caesar's favor showers down greatness on his friends, that will raise me to Rome's first honors. If I give up Cato, I can claim my reward in his captive daughter. Ah, Syphax comes!

ACT I, Scene 3

Setting: A large open hall in the Governor's Palace of Utica.

Cast: SYPHAX, SEMPRONIUS

At Rise: SEMPRONIUS pacing when SYPHAX enters and approaches him.

***

SYPHAX

Sempronius, all is ready, I've tested my Numidians, man by man, and find them ripe for a revolt! They all complain aloud of Cato's harsh discipline, and wait for the command to change their master.

SEMPRONIUS

Believe me, Syphax, there's no time to waste; even while

we speak our conqueror gathers ground on us every moment. You do not know Caesar's soul. He rushes from war to war; in vain has nature formed mountains and oceans to oppose his passage. He bounds over them all! Just one day more and the victor will be thundering at our gates. But tell me, have you won over young Juba yet?

SYPHAX

He's lost, he's lost, Sempronius. All his thoughts are full of Cato's virtues. But I'll try once more; any moment I expect him here. If I can just subdue his stubborn principles of faith and honor.

SEMPRONIUS

Be sure to press every motive upon him. Juba's surrender, since his father's death, would put all of Africa into Caesar's hands.

SYPHAX

But is it true, Sempronius, that the senate is called together? Gods, we must be cautious! Cato has piercing eyes, and will discern our frauds, unless they're covered thick with art.

SEMPRONIUS

Good Syphax, I'll conceal my thoughts in passion, it's the surest way. I'll bellow out for Rome and for my country, and speak ill of Caesar until I shake the senate.

SYPHAX

In truth, you are able to teach that wily African deceit!

SEMPRONIUS

Once more, be sure to try your skills on Juba. Meanwhile I'll hasten to my Roman soldiers and inflame the mutiny until they break out on Cato. Remember, Syphax, we must work in haste. Think of what anxious moments pass between the birth of plots, and their last fatal moments. Oh! It's a dreadful interval of time, filled with horror, and big with death! Destruction hangs on every word we speak, on every thought, until the concluding stroke determines all, and closes our design.

(SEMPRONIUS exits)

SYPHAX

(alone)

I'll try to reason with that headstrong youth, and make him disdain Cato. The time is short, Caesar comes rushing on us, but hold! Young Juba sees me, and approaches.

ACT I, Scene 4

Setting: A large open hall in the Governor's Palace of Utica.

Cast: JUBA, SYPHAX

At Rise: SYPHAX is alone when JUBA enters.

***

JUBA

Syphax, I'm glad to see you alone. Lately, I have observed your looks have fallen. Tell me, what are the thoughts that knit your brow in frowns, and turn your eye coldly on your prince?

SYPHAX

It is not my talent to conceal my thoughts when discontent sits heavy on my heart. I don't that much

Roman in me.

JUBA

Why do you speak so ungenerously against the lords of the world? Don't you see mankind fall down before them, and accept the force of their superior virtue? Is there a nation in the wilds of Africa that does not tremble at the Roman name?

SYPHAX

Gods! Where's the worth that sets this people up above your own Numidian sons! Do Roman arms fly their javelins swifter to its mark? Who instructs their steeds better than our Africans? Or better guides the embattled elephant laden for war? These, these are arts, my prince, in which your people do not stoop to Rome!

JUBA

These are all virtues of a meaner rank, perfections that are placed in bones and nerves. A Roman soul is bent on higher views; to civilize the rude, unpolished world, and bring it under the restraint of laws. To make men mild, and sociable to each other; to cultivate the wild savage with wisdom, and liberal arts. The embellishments of life, virtues like these, make human nature shine, and break our fierce barbarians into men.

SYPHAX

Patience, kind heavens! Excuse an old man's warmth.

What are these wondrous arts, this Roman polish, that render man so tame? Are they not only to disguise our true passions? Are they to change us into other creatures, other than what our nature and the gods created us to be?

JUBA

You wouldn't speak so if you turned your eyes to Cato! Then you would see the godlike height Roman virtues have lifted up mortal man! While good, and just for his friends, he works against himself; renouncing sleep, and rest, and food, he strives with thirst and hunger, toil and heat. And when his fortune sets before him all the pomp and pleasures that his soul can wish, his rigid virtue will accept of none of it.

SYPHAX

Believe me, prince, there's not an African that travels our vast Numidian deserts in quest of prey, living upon his bow, that does not practice these virtues. Coarse are his meals, at the running stream he quenches his thirst, he toils all the day, and at the approach of night he throws himself down on the first river bank and rests his head upon a rock until morning. Then rises fresh to pursue his game again.

JUBA

Your prejudices, Syphax, don't discern what virtues grow from ignorance or choice, nor how the hero differs from the brute. Where can we find a man that bears affliction, great and majestic in his griefs, like Cato? Heavens! With what strength, what steadiness of mind, he triumphs over all his sufferings! He rises above a load of woes, and thanks the gods that throw the weight upon him!

SYPHAX

It is pride, rank pride, and haughtiness of soul; I think the Romans call it being a "stoic." If your royal father had not thought so highly of Roman virtue, and of Cato's cause, he would have not fallen by a slave's hand, so ingloriously.

JUBA

Why do you bring up my sorrows? My father's name brings tears into my eyes.

SYPHAX

So that you might profit by your father's misfortunes!

JUBA

What would you have me do?

SYPHAX

Abandon Cato.

JUBA

Syphax, I would be twice an orphan by such a loss!

SYPHAX

Ah ha, there's the tie that binds you! You long to call him father. Marcia's charms work in your heart, and plead for Cato. No wonder you're deaf to all I say.

JUBA

Syphax, your zeal becomes too much. I've permitted you to talk freely until now; but learn to keep it in, before it takes more freedom than I'll give it.

SYPHAX

Sir, your great father never treated me so, but alas, he's dead! Can you ever forget the repeated blessings you drew from him in your last farewell? I cannot forget, before he parted, holding my hand, his eyes full of tears, crying, "Be careful of my son!" His grief swelled up so high, he could utter no more.

JUBA

Syphax, your story melts away my soul. He was the best of fathers! How can I discharge the gratitude I owe him?

SYPHAX

By laying up his counsels in your heart.

JUBA

His counsels did require me to yield to your directions. Syphax, scold me in severest terms, vent all your passions, and I'll stand it, calm and unruffled as a summer sea.

SYPHAX

Alas, my prince, I'll guide you to safety.

JUBA

I do believe you will; but how?

SYPHAX

Cast off the fate that follows Caesar's foes.

JUBA

My father would not do so.

SYPHAX

And therefore he died.

JUBA

Better to die ten thousand, thousand deaths, than wound my honor.

SYPHAX

Your honor? Or should you say your love?

JUBA

Syphax, I've promised to withhold my temper. Why would you press me to confess a flame I have long stifled?

SYPHAX

Believe me, prince, though love is hard to conquer, it's easy to divert its force. Absence might cure it, or a second mistress. Why not light another flame, and put this one out? The glowing dames of Africa's courts have faces finished with more exalted charms. Were you with these, my prince, you would soon forget the pale beauties of the north.

JUBA

It is not a set of features, or complexion that I admire.

Beauty soon grows familiar to the lover, and fades in his eyes. The virtuous Marcia towers above her sex. True, she is fair, oh how divinely fair! But still the lovely maid improves her charms with inward greatness. Cato's soul shines out in everything she says and does, while mildness dwells in her looks. Her grace softens the rigor of her father's virtue.

SYPHAX

But on my knees I beg you would consider —

JUBA

- Hah! Syphax, is this not she? She comes this way, and with Lucia, Lucius's fair daughter. My heart beats quick — please, Syphax, leave me.

SYPHAX

(bows and begins to exits)

As you wish, my prince.

(aside)

Ten thousand curses on them both! This woman undoes all I've been laboring for with a single glance!

(SYPHAX exits)

ACT I, Scene 5

Setting: A large open hall in the Governor's Palace of Utica.

Cast: JUBA, MARCIA

At Rise: JUBA is alone when MARCIA enters.

***

JUBA

Hail, charming maid! How your beauty smooths the face of war, and makes even horror smile! At the sight of you my heart shakes off its sorrows and for a while even forgets the approach of Caesar.

MARCIA

I should be grieved, young prince, to think my presence unbent your thoughts, while our victorious foe calls you to the field.

JUBA

Marcia, let me hope your gentle wishes follow me to battle! The thought will give new vigor to my arm, and add weight to my falling sword.

MARCIA

My wishes always follow the friends of Rome, the glorious cause of virtue, and men approved of by the gods and Cato.

JUBA

That I may deserve your precious cares, I'll gaze forever on your godlike father, transplanting, one by one, into my life, his bright perfections, until I shine like him.

MARCIA

My father would never lay out his great soul at a time like this, and waste such precious moments.

JUBA

Your rebuke is just, virtuous maid. I'll hasten to my troops, and fire their souls with Cato's virtue! If ever I lead them to the field, when all the war shall rage around me, then will I think of you! Oh lovely maid, then will I think of you! And, remember what glorious deeds should grace the man, who hopes for Marcia's love.

(JUBA exits)

ACT I, Scene 6

Setting: A large open hall in the Governor's Palace of Utica.

Cast: LUCIA, MARCIA

At Rise: LUCIA enters as JUBA exits.

***

LUCIA

Marcia, you were too severe! How could you reprimand the young prince, and drive him away so bitterly? A prince that loves, and dotes on you to death?

MARCIA

That is why I sent him from me, Lucia. His voice, his looks, and honest soul speak all so movingly on his behalf, I dare not trust myself to hear him talk.

LUCIA

Why would you fight against so sweet a passion, and harden your heart to such a world of charms?

MARCIA

Lucia! How can I lose myself in love, when Cato's life is at stake? Caesar comes armed with terror and revenge, and aims his thunder at my father's head. Shouldn't that swallow up my other cares?

LUCIA

For sure, nature formed me of her softest mold, enfeebled my soul with tender passions, and sunk me even below my own weak sex. Pity and love, by turns, oppress my heart.

MARCIA

Lucia, unburden all your cares on me, and let me share your distress. Tell me who raises up this conflict in you?

LUCIA

I blush to name them, they're Marcia's brothers, the sons of Cato.

MARCIA

Yes, they have often revealed their passion to me. But tell me, who do you favor most? I long to know, and yet I dread to hear it.

LUCIA

Which do you wish for?

MARCIA

For neither -and yet for both. But tell me, which of them is Lucia's choice?

LUCIA

Marcia, they are both high in my esteem. But in my love — why will you make me name him? It's a blind and foolish passion-

MARCIA

-Oh Lucia, tell me which one I must call my happy brother?

LUCIA

What if it were Portius, could you blame my choice? Oh Portius, you have stolen my soul away! With such a graceful tenderness he loves. And breathes the softest, most sincerest vows! Truth, and manly sweetness dwell forever on his tongue.

(pause)

Marcus is overwarm, his fond complaints have so much passion in them, I hear him with a secret kind of horror, and tremble at his temper.

MARCIA

That poor youth! Lucia, you do not know half the love

he holds for you! Whenever he speaks of you, his heart's in flames. He sends out all his soul in every word, and thinks, and talks, and looks like one transported. Your coldness will raise storms in his afflicted bosom! I dread the consequence.

LUCIA

You seem to plead against your brother Portius.

MARCIA

Heaven forbid! Had Portius been the unsuccessful lover, I would have given him the same compassion.

LUCIA

Was ever a new love distressed like mine?! Portius often falls in tears before me, as if he mourned his rival's success. Then bids me to hide the motions of my heart; he fears the sad effects that it would have on Marcus.

MARCIA

He does not want to plunge his brother in despair; but waits for happier times, and kinder moments.

LUCIA

And what of me! I always find myself involved in endless griefs. Was I born to sow dissension in the hearts of brothers? It cuts into my soul!

MARCIA

Lucia, let us not aggravate our sorrows, but leave the

event of things to the gods. Our lives may still grow bright, and smile with happier hours.

(exeunt MARCIA and LUCIA)

ACT I, Scene 7

Setting: The Senate.

Cast: SEMPRONIUS, LUCIUS, CATO, MARCUS, SENATE MEMBER #1, SENATE MEMBER #2, SENATE MEMBER #3

At Rise: SEMPRONIUS standing addressing LUCIUS, MARCUS, SENATE MEMBER #1, SENATE MEMBER #2, SENATE MEMBER #3, who are all seated. CATO is not yet on stage.

***

SEMPRONIUS

Rome still survives in this assembled senate! Let us remember we are Cato's friends, and act like men who deserve that glorious title.

LUCIUS

Cato will soon be here, and reveal to us the motive of our
meeting. Hark! He comes!

(the sound of trumpets is heard)
May all the gods of Rome direct him!

(enter CATO)

CATO

Fathers, we meet once again in council. Caesar's
approach has summoned us together, and Rome awaits
her fate. How will we treat this bold, aspiring man?
Success still follows him, and backs his crimes. Our civil
war gave him Rome; Egypt has since received his yoke,
and the whole Nile is Caesar's! It is time we must choose
the course we take. Fathers, speak your thoughts, are they
still fixed to fight to the last? Or have your hearts been
subdued by time? Sempronius, speak.

SEMPRONIUS

My voice is still for war! We face slavery or death, does
a Roman senate need to debate which to choose? No, let
us rise at once, gird our swords, and attack the foe, break
through his legions, and charge upon him. Perhaps some
arm, more lucky than the rest, may reach his heart, and
free the world from bondage. Rise, fathers, rise! Rome
demands your help. Rise, and revenge her slaughtered
citizens, or share their fate! The corpses of half her

senate manure the fields of Thessaly, while we sit here in cold debates. Should we sacrifice our lives to honor, or squander them in chains? Rise up, for shame! Our murdered brothers point at their wounds, and cry aloud — to battle!

CATO

Let us not follow your zeal beyond the bounds of reason. True fortitude is seen in exploits that justice warrants, and wisdom guides. All else is frenzy and distraction. We should not ignore the lives of those who draw the sword in Rome's defense, they are entrusted to our care! Should we lead them to a field of slaughter? The world might say we poured out the blood of thousands to grace our fall, and make our ruin glorious. Lucius, what is your opinion?

LUCIUS

I must confess, my thoughts have turned to peace. Our quarrels have already filled the world with widows and orphans. Earth's remotest regions lie half abandoned because of the feuds of Rome. It is time to sheath the sword, and spare mankind. It is not Caesar, but the gods, my fathers, the gods work against us. We have already shown our love for Rome, let us now show submission to the gods. Arms have no farther use. Our country's cause now tugs them from our hands, and begs us not to delight in the shedding of Roman blood. What men could do is done already. If Rome must fall, heaven and Earth will witness that we are innocent.

SEMPRONIUS
(leaning in to whisper to CATO)
Smooth speech and mild behavior often conceal a traitor.
All is not right. Cato, beware of Lucius.

CATO
Fathers, I cannot believe our affairs have grown so
desperate. We have bulwarks all around us. Within our
walls are troops hardened to fight in Africa's heat,
seasoned to the sun. Numidia's spacious kingdom lies
behind us, ready to rise at its young prince's call. While
there is hope, do not distrust the gods; but wait at least
until Caesar's approach forces us to yield. It will never
be too late to put on chains, and kneel to a conqueror.
Why should Rome fall a moment before her time! No, let
us draw her time of freedom out to its full length. In my
judgement, one day, one hour of liberty is worth a whole
eternity in bondage.

(enter MARCUS)

MARCUS
Fathers, a messenger from Caesar's camp has just
arrived, and with him comes old Decius, the Roman
knight. He seems to be impatience, and demands to
speak with Cato.

CATO
By your permission, fathers, let him enter.

(SENATORS respond in the positive, nodding. Exit
Marcus)

CATO

(speaking to the group)

Decius was once my friend, but other prospects have
loosened those ties, and bound him to Caesar. His
message may determine our resolves.

ACT I, Scene 8

Setting: The Senate.

Cast: SEMPRONIUS, LUCIUS, CATO, MARCUS, SENATE MEMBER #1, SENATE MEMBER #2, SENATE MEMBER #3, DECIUS

At Rise: ALL are seated, except CATO who is standing proudly waiting for DECIUS

***

DECIUS

Caesar sends health to Cato!

CATO

Could he send it to Cato's murdered friends? It would be welcome. (pause) Are not your orders to address the senate?

DECIUS

No, my business is with you.

(DECIUS gestures CATO to walk to the side with him,
and CATO walks with DECIUS)

Cato, Caesar sees the straits to which you've been driven;
and, as he knows your worth, is concerned for your life.

CATO

My life is grafted on the fate of Rome. If he wants to save
Cato, he must spare his country. Tell your dictator that
Cato disdains a life which he has power to offer.

DECIUS

Rome and her senators submit to Caesar. The generals
and consuls who checked his conquests and denied his
triumphs are no more. The time has come for Cato to be
Caesar's friend.

CATO

And for those very reasons I will not submit!

DECIUS

Cato, I have orders to reason with you, from friend to
friend. Think of the storm that gathers over your head.
Make your peace with Caesar. Rome will rejoice, and cast
its eyes on Cato as the second of mankind.

CATO

No more! I will not think of life on such conditions.

DECIUS

Caesar is well acquainted with your virtues. Let him know the price of your friendship; name any terms.

CATO

Any terms? Tell him to disband his legions, restore Rome to liberty, submit his actions to public censure, and stand the judgment of a Roman senate. When he does these things, Cato will be his friend.

DECIUS

Cato, the world talks loudly of your wisdom, but —

CATO

- Even more, although I have never spoken to clear the guilty, I will speak in his favor, and attempt to gain his pardon from the people.

DECIUS

Ah, a style like this becomes a conqueror.

CATO

Decius, a style like this becomes a Roman.

DECIUS

What is a Roman that is Caesar's foe?

CATO

Greater than Caesar; he's a friend to virtue!

DECIUS

Consider, Cato, you're in Utica, at the head of your own little senate. You don't thunder in the capitol now, with all the mouths of Rome to second you.

CATO

It was Caesar's sword that thinned the ranks of Rome's senate and made it little. But your dazzled eyes can only see him in a false light. If you viewed him as he is, you would see murder, treason, sacrilege, and crimes that strike at my soul with horror just to name them. I know you look on me as a wretch, covered with misfortunes, but, by the gods I swear, millions of worlds will never buy me to be like Caesar!

DECIUS

Does Cato send this answer back to Caesar, for all his generous favors, and offer of friendship?

CATO

His favors mean nothing to me; the gods take care of Cato! If Caesar wants to show the generosity of his soul, ask him to care for my friends, and make good use of his ill-gotten power by sheltering men much better than himself.

DECIUS

Cato, do not forget you are still just a man, why do you rush to your own destruction? (waits for a response, not truly expecting one) But I have done what I could. When I relate the tale of this unhappy encounter, all of Rome will be in tears.

(exit DECIUS)

ACT I, Scene 9

Setting: The Senate.

Cast: SEMPRONIUS, LUCIUS, CATO, MARCUS, SENATE MEMBER #1, SENATE MEMBER #2, SENATE MEMBER #3

At Rise: CATO walks over to look outside, ALL are seated, until SEMPRONIUS

***

SEMPRONIUS

Cato, we thank you! The mighty, immortal Rome speaks in your voice, your very soul breathes liberty. Caesar will shrink to hear your words, and shudder in the midst of all his conquests.

LUCIUS

The senate owes its gratitude to Cato, who with so great a soul consults its safety, and guards our lives, while he neglects his own.

SEMPRONIUS

Lucius, you seem so fond of life; but what is life? It is to walk about, and breathe fresh air, or gaze upon the sun? It is to be free. When liberty is gone, life grows trite, and loses its savor. Oh, if only my dying hand could lodge a sword in Caesar's bosom, and revenge my country! By the heavens I could enjoy the pangs of death and smile in agony!

LUCIUS

Others, perhaps, may serve their country with as warm a zeal, without so much rage.

SEMPRONIUS

This sober conduct is a mighty virtue in lukewarm patriots.

CATO
(turns quickly to address SEMRONIUS)
Enough! No more, Sempronius. All here are friends to Rome, and to each other. Let us not weaken still the weaker side by our divisions.

SEMPRONIUS

Cato, my resentments are sacrificed to Rome, I stand

reproved.

CATO

Fathers, it is time you come to a resolve.

LUCIUS

Cato, we all accept your opinion; we ought to hold out until terms arrive.

SEMPRONIUS

We ought to hold out until death, but, Cato, my voice is drowned out by the senate's.

CATO

Then let us rise, my friends, and strive to fill this little pause of life with Roman bravery and all the virtues we can crowd into it; so heaven may say, it ought to be prolonged. Fathers, farewell! The young Numidian prince comes forward, and expects to know our counsels.

ACT II, Scene 1

Setting: A large open hall in the Governor's Palace of Utica.

Cast: CATO, JUBA

At Rise: CATO and JUBA already onstage in discussion.

***

CATO

Juba, the senate has resolved that, until time gives us better prospects, we should keep the sword unsheathed, and turn its edge on Caesar.

JUBA

The resolution fits a Roman senate. But, Cato, lend me your patience, and allow a young man to speak. My father, some days before his death, ordered me to march for

Utica. He wept over me, pressed me in his aged arms, and, as his griefs gave way said, "My son, whatever fortune shall befall your father, be Cato's friend. He'll train you in great and virtuous deeds. Observe him well and you will shun misfortunes, or will learn to bear them."

CATO

Juba, your father was a worthy prince, and merited a better fate; but heaven thought otherwise.

JUBA

My father's fate fills my eyes with tears.

CATO

It is an honest sorrow.

JUBA

The kings of Africa, that rule behind the hidden sources of the Nile, sought him for their friend. Often their ambassadors appeared, laden with gifts, and filled the courts of Zama.

CATO

I am no stranger to your father's greatness.

JUBA

I boast about his greatness, only to point out new alliances to you, to court the assistance of his powerful friends. If they knew you, our remotest kings would pour embattled multitudes about you. They would darken all our plains, doubling the horror of the war, and making death more grim.

CATO

Do you think I would flee from the sword of Caesar? To live like Hannibal, seeking relief from court to court, wandering up and down Africa like a beggar!

JUBA

Cato, perhaps I was too forward, but I merely wish to preserve a life of so much value. My heart is wounded when I see such virtue afflicted by the weight of such misfortunes.

CATO

The nobleness of your soul obliges me. But know, young prince, that valor soars above what the world calls misfortune. These are not ills; if they were, they would never fall on heaven's first favorites. The gods work up storms around us, that give mankind occasion to exert their hidden strength, and throw into practice virtues, which shun the day, and lie concealed in the calms of life.

JUBA

I'm charmed whenever you talk! I pant for virtue! All my soul endeavors at perfection.

CATO

Do you love abstinence and toil? They are painstaking virtues! Learn them from Cato, but success and fortune you must learn from Caesar. Tell me your wish, young prince; do not make my ear a stranger to your thoughts.

JUBA

They are too extravagant! Let me keep them hidden.

CATO

What could you ask that I would refuse?

JUBA

I'm afraid to name it. Marcia inherits all her father's virtue.

CATO

What is it you say?

JUBA

Cato, you have a daughter -

CATO

- Good bye, young prince. I will not listen to any word that will lessen my esteem in you. Remember the hand of fate is over us. It is not time to talk of these things, but of chains or conquest, liberty or death.

(CATO exits)

ACT II, Scene 2

Setting: A large open hall in the Governor's Palace of Utica.

Cast: SYPHAX, JUBA

At Rise: JUBA standing looking very sad when SYPHAX enters.

***

SYPHAX

What is this, my prince?! You seem covered with confusion. You look as if our stern philosopher had just scolded you.

JUBA

Syphax, I'm undone!

SYPHAX

I know it well.

JUBA

Cato thinks unkindly of me.

SYPHAX

Then so will all of mankind.

JUBA

I've opened the weakness of my soul to him - my love for Marcia.

SYPHAX

You imagined Cato to be the proper person to trust a love tale with?

JUBA

Oh! I could pierce my heart, my foolish heart! Was there ever a wretch like me?

SYPHAX

Alas! my prince, how you've changed of late! I've known you to rise, before the sun, to beat the thicket where the tiger slept, or seek the lion in his dreadful haunts. How you loved to rouse them to the chase!

JUBA

Please, no more!

SYPHAX

How the old king would smile to see you with your shaggy spoils about your shoulders!

JUBA

Syphax, Cato is displeased; I've lost Marcia forever!

SYPHAX

Young prince, I can still give you good advice. Marcia might still be yours.

JUBA

What is this you say, Syphax?

SYPHAX

Marcia might still be yours.

JUBA

How, dear Syphax?

SYPHAX

How? Do you not command Numidia's troops, mounted on steeds swifter than the wind?

JUBA

It is true.

SYPHAX

Then give the word and we'll snatch this damsel up, and fly off with her!

JUBA

How can such dishonest thoughts rise up in a man?!
Would you entice me to do an act that would destroy my
honor?

SYPHAX

Gods! I could tear my hair out to hear you talk! Honor's
a fine imaginary notion, but it's only meant to draw in
unexperienced men to real mischiefs while they hunt a
shadow.

JUBA

You would degrade your prince into a ruffian?

SYPHAX

The ancestors of the great men, whose virtues you
admire, were all such ruffians. This dread of nations,
this almighty Rome, was founded on a rape. Your Scipio,
Caesars, Pompey, and your Cato, these gods on earth, are
all the illegitimate brood of ravished maids.

JUBA

Syphax, I fear that head of yours abounds too much in our
Numidian trickeries.

SYPHAX

Indeed, my prince, you do not know the world. Your
youth admires the swellings of a Roman soul.

JUBA

If knowledge of the world makes man deceitful, then may
I forever live in ignorance!

SYPHAX

Go, go, you're young.

JUBA

(looking up towards the sky)

Gods! I cannot allow this arrogance to go unanswered!

(turns to speak to SYPHAX again)

You are a traitor, a false old traitor!

SYPHAX

(aside, to himself)

I have gone too far.

JUBA

Cato will know the wickedness of your soul!

SYPHAX

(aside, to himself)

I must appease this storm, or perish in it.

(to JUBA)

Young prince, behold these locks that have grown white
beneath a helmet in your father's battles.

JUBA

Those locks will not protect your insolence!

SYPHAX

Must one rash word, the infirmity of age, throw down the merit of my better years? Is this to be my reward for a whole life of service?

JUBA

Is it because the throne of my forefathers still stands unfilled? That the head Numidia's crown will hang on remains doubtful? Is this why you treat your prince with scorn?

SYPHAX

Why will you tear my heart with such expressions? Does not old Syphax follow you to war? Is it not to shed my last poor drop of blood in your defense?

JUBA

Syphax, no more! I will not hear you talk.

SYPHAX

Not hear me talk?! When my faith to Juba, my master's son, is called in question? My prince may strike me dead, but while I live I must not hold my tongue.

JUBA

You know the way into my heart too well, I do believe you are loyal to your prince.

SYPHAX

What greater instance can I give? I've offered to do an action, that my soul abhors, to gain you the one you love, at any price.

JUBA

Was that your motive? I may have been too hasty.

SYPHAX

And for this my prince has called me traitor.

JUBA

Surely you are mistaken; I did not call you so.

SYPHAX

You did indeed, my prince, you called me a traitor. Nay, farther, you threatened you'd complain to Cato of it. Would you complain to Cato that Syphax loves you, and would sacrifice his life, and more, his honor, in your service?

JUBA

Syphax, I know you love me, but indeed your zeal for me carried you too far. Honor's sacred tie, the law of kings, the noble mind's distinguishing perfection ought not to be sported with.

SYPHAX

By heavens! I'm ravished when you talk so! I've been used to thinking a blind zeal was proper to serve my king. A ruling principle that ought to burn and quench all others in a subject's heart.

JUBA

Syphax, Numidia's grown to be a scorn among the nations for her breach of public vows. Our Punic faith is infamous, and branded to a proverb. Let us join our cares, to purge away our country's crimes, and clear her reputation.

SYPHAX

Believe me, prince, you make old Syphax weep to hear you talk — but with tears of joy. If ever your father's crown adorns your brows, Numidia will be blessed by Cato's lectures.

JUBA

Syphax, we'll mutually forget the warmth of youth, and frowardness of age. If ever the royal staff comes into my hand, Syphax shall stand second in my kingdom.

SYPHAX

Why will you overwhelm my age with kindness? My joy grows burdensome.

JUBA

Syphax, farewell. I'll try to find some cause that may set me right in Cato's thoughts. I'd rather have that one man approve my deeds, than a world of my admirers.

(JUBA exits)

SYPHAX

(alone)

Young men soon give, and soon forget insults, but old age
is slow in both. A "false old traitor"! Those words, rash
boy, will cost you dearly. My heart still had some foolish
fondness for you, but I give it to the wind now. Caesar, I
am altogether yours!

ACT II, Scene 3

Setting: A large open hall in the Governor's Palace of Utica.

Cast: SYPHAX, SEMPRONIUS

At Rise: SYPHAX already in position when SEMPRONIUS enters.

***

SYPHAX

So, Sempronius, Cato's little senate has resolved to wait for the fury of a siege before it yields.

SEMPRONIUS

Syphax, we were both on the verge of fate. Lucius declared for peace, and terms were offered to Cato by a messenger from Caesar. Should they submit, our designs are ripe, but we both must perish in the common wreck.

SYPHAX

But how stands Cato?

SEMPRONIUS

As Mount Atlas; while storms thunder on its brows, and oceans break at its feet, it stands unmoved, and glories in its height. Such is that haughty man; his towering soul, midst all the shocks and injuries of fortune, rises superior, and looks down on Caesar.

SYPHAX

Who was this messenger?

SEMPRONIUS

I spoke with him, and he will let the victor know that Syphax and Sempronius are his friends. Let me ask you, is Juba fixed?

SYPHAX

Yes, but it's Cato I've tried the force of every reason on, but all are in vain, he scorns them all.

SEMPRONIUS

No matter, we shall do without him. Syphax, I hope you have forsaken Juba's cause, and wish Marcia was mine.

SYPHAX

May she be yours as fast as you would have her!

SEMPRONIUS

Syphax, I love that woman; though I curse her and myself, yet, I love her.

SYPHAX

Persuade Cato to give up Utica, and Caesar will never refuse you such a trifle request. Are your troops prepared for a revolt?

SEMPRONIUS

All, all is ready, the rebel leaders are our friends, they spread murmurs and discontents among the soldiers. Within the hour they will storm the senate.

SYPHAX

Meanwhile I'll draw up my Numidian troops within the square to exercise their arms, and as I see fit, will support you. I laugh to think how your unshaken Cato will look aghast, while destruction pours in upon him from every side.

(exeunt SEMPRONIUS and SYPHAX)

ACT II, Scene 4

Setting: A large open hall in the Governor's Palace of Utica.

Cast: MARCUS, PORTIUS

At Rise: MARCUS and PORTIUS enter already in the midst of speaking.

***

MARCUS

I thank my stars, I did not stumble about the wilds of life before I could find a friend like you. Nature first pointed you out to me, and through instinct, it grew up into friendship.

PORTIUS

Marcus, the friendships of the world are often

confederacies in vice, or leagues of pleasure. Ours has virtue for its basis, and such a friendship ends only with life.

MARCUS

Portius, you know my soul in all its weakness, so please understand its tender side, that longs to indulge in love.

PORTIUS

When love's well-timed, the strong, the virtuous, and the wise, sink in its soft captivity together. I would not ask you to dismiss your passion, it would be in vain, but to suppress its force, until better times may make it look more graceful.

MARCUS

You talk like one who never felt the impatient throbs of a soul, that pants, and reaches for a distant good. A lover does not live by vulgar time. Believe me, Portius, in my Lucia's absence life hangs upon me, and becomes a burden. And yet, when I behold the charming maid, I'm ten times more undone, while hope and fear, and grief, and rage, and love, rise up at once.

PORTIUS

What can your friend do to help?

MARCUS

Portius, you often enjoyed the fair one's presence. Undertake my cause, and plead it to her with all the strength and heat our friendship can inspire. Tell her your brother languishes to death, and withers in his bloom. That he forgets his sleep, and loathes his food. That youth, and health, and war, are joyless to him.

PORTIUS

Marcus, I beg you not to ask me to do something that suits me so poorly.

MARCUS

Will you just watch me sink in my woes? Will you not reach out a friendly arm, to raise me from this plunge of sorrows?

PORTIUS

Marcus, you cannot ask what I'd refuse. Believe me, I've a thousand reasons—

MARCUS

-I know you'll say my passion's out of season; that Cato's misfortunes should drive it from my thoughts. But what's all this to one that loves like me? Oh Portius, from my soul, I wish you knew yourself what it is to love! Then you would pity your brother.

PORTIUS

(aside, speaking to himself)

What should I do? If I disclose my passion for her, our friendship will be at an end. If I conceal it, the world will call me untruthful to my brother.

MARCUS

But see where Lucia enjoys the noon-day breeze amid the cool of the high marble arch! Observe her, Portius! That face, that shape, those eyes, that heavenly beauty! Observe her well, and blame me if you can.

PORTIUS

She sees us, she comes this way-

MARCUS

— I'll withdraw, and leave you for awhile. Remember, Portius, your brother's life depends upon your tongue.

(MARCUS exits)

ACT II, Scene 5

Setting: A large open hall in the Governor's Palace of Utica.

Cast: LUCIA, PORTIUS

At Rise: PORTIUS stands waiting LUCIA's approach.

***

LUCIA

Did I not see your brother Marcus here? Why did he leave, and shun my presence?

PORTIUS

Oh Lucia! Language is too faint to show his love for you; it preys upon his very life. His passions and his virtues are confused, and mixed together in so wild a tumult, that the whole man is quite disfigured in him. Heavens! Would anyone think it was possible for love to make such ravage in a noble soul! Lucia, I'm distressed! My heart bleeds even while I stand in your presence, a secret grief comes over my thoughts, though you smile upon me.

LUCIA

How will you guard your honor in the shock of love and friendship? Think, my Portius, think of how our mutual bliss would raise your brother's griefs to new heights, perhaps even destroy him.

PORTIUS

That poor youth! What do you think, my Lucia? His generous, open heart has begged me, his rival, to petition for him. Do not strike him dead with a denial, but cheer his soul with the faint glimmer of a doubtful hope —

LUCIA

-No, Portius, no! I see your sister's tears, your father's anguish, and your brother's death, in the pursuit of our ill-fated love. And, Portius, here I swear, to heaven I swear, to heaven and all the powers that judge mankind, never to mix my hand with yours while such a cloud of mischiefs hangs over us. I will forget our love, and drive you out of my thoughts, as far as I am able.

PORTIUS

What have you said! Please take back those hasty words, or I am lost forever.

LUCIA

The vow has already passed my lips. The gods have heard it, and it is sealed in heaven. May all the vengeance that was ever poured on a perjured head, overwhelm me if I break it!

PORTIUS

I look upon you now like one just blasted by a strike from heaven!

LUCIA

At length I've acted my part. I feel the woman breaking in upon me, and melt my heart! My tears will flow. But oh, I'll think no more! The hand of fate has torn you from me, and I must forget you.

PORTIUS

Cold-hearted, cruel maid!

LUCIA

Stop those sounds, those killing sounds! Why do you frown upon me? The gods forbid us to indulge our love, but I cannot bear your hate, and live!

PORTIUS

Talk not of love, you never knew its force. I've been deluded, led into a dream of bliss. Oh Lucia, your dreadful vow still sounds in my ears. What shall I say or do? Quick, let us part! — ah, she faints!

(LUCIA faints)

PORTIUS

Wretch that I am! What has my rashness done? Lucia, your injured innocence! Awake, my Lucia, or I'll rush on my sword to join you. But hah! she moves! Life wanders through her face, and lights up every charm.

LUCIA

Oh Portius, was it well to frown on her that lives by your smile? To call in doubt the faith of one that loves you more than any woman ever loved!

(gathering her thoughts)
What am I saying? My senses forget the vow in which my soul is bound. Destruction stands between us! We must part.

PORTIUS

Do not say the words again. My thoughts will turn to madness at the sound!

LUCIA

What would you have me do? Consider the train of ills our love would draw behind it. Think, Portius, think, would you see your brother stabbed at his heart, storming at heaven and you?!

PORTIUS

To my eternal grief, I must accept the sentence that

destroys me. The mist that hung about my mind, clears up. Loveliest of women! heaven is in your soul, beauty and virtue shine forever around you! You are all divine!

LUCIA

Portius, no more! Your words shoot through my heart, melt my resolve, and turn me all to love. Why are those tears of fondness in your eyes? It softens me too much — farewell, my Portius.

PORTIUS

Stay, Lucia stay!

LUCIA

Have I not sworn?! Farewell, Portius.

PORTIUS

You must not go!

LUCIA

If the firm Portius shakes to hear of parting, think how I suffer!

PORTIUS

It's true; unruffled I've met the accidents of life, but here such an unexpected storm of ills falls on me, it beats down all my strength. I cannot bear it. We must not part.

LUCIA

Not part?! Are there not heavens, and gods, and thunder over us?! (pause) — But see! your brother Marcus comes this way! I must leave. Once more, farewell, farewell, and know that there was never a love, or grief, like mine.

(LUCIA exits)

ACT II, Scene 6

Setting: A large open hall in the Governor's Palace of Utica.

Cast: MARCUS, PORTIUS

At Rise: PORTIUS stands waiting for MARCUS

***

MARCUS

Portius, what hope do I have? Am I doomed to life or death?

PORTIUS

What would you have me say?

MARCUS

What is this pondering posture? You look like someone amazed and terrified.

PORTIUS

I have reason to.

MARCUS

Your downcast looks tell me my fate. There's no need to ask what success my cause has found.

PORTIUS

I'm grieved I undertook it.

MARCUS

That harsh maid insults my heart, my aching heart! If only I could cast her from my thoughts forever!

PORTIUS

Away! Lucia has sworn never to think of love, but has compassion for you, she pities you.

MARCUS

Pities me?! What is compassion without love? I was a fool to choose so cold a friend to urge my cause! Please tell me what language did you use to gain this mighty boon? She pities me!

PORTIUS

Marcus, no more! Do I deserve this treatment?

MARCUS

What have I said! Oh Portius, forgive me! My soul was provoked — but, wait! What is that shout, big with the sounds of war?

PORTIUS

A second, louder yet, and comes near upon us.

MARCUS

Oh, for some glorious cause to fall in battle! Lucia, you have undone me! Your disdain has broken my heart. Only death will give me ease.

PORTIUS

Quick, let us go; who knows if Cato's life is secure. Marcus, I am warmed, my heart leaps at the trumpet's voice, and burns for glory.

(exeunt MARCUS and PORTIUS)

ACT III, Scene 1

Setting: Open Air Square.

Cast: SEMPRONIUS, MUTINY LEADER, SOLDIER #1 to #3

At Rise: SEMPRONIUS is addressing MUTINY LEADER and SOLDIER #1 to #3

***

SEMPRONIUS
(to MUTINY LEADER)

The winds are raised, and the storm blows high! Take care, my friends, keep it up in its full fury until it has spent itself on Cato's head. Meanwhile I'll stay among his friends, and seem one of them, that whatever may happen, my friends and fellow-soldiers may be safe.

MUTINY LEADER
(to GROUP)

We all are safe, Sempronius is our friend. Sempronius is as brave a man as Cato. But, wait! Cato comes this way!

(to SEMPRONIUS)

Be bold to him, Sempronius. Be sure you beat him down, and bind him fast. This day will end our toils, and give us rest! (to GROUP) Fear nothing, for Sempronius is our friend.

ACT III, Scene 2

Setting: Open Air Square.

Cast: SEMPRONIUS, MUTINY LEADER, SOLDIER #1 to #3, CATO, LUCIUS

At Rise: SEMPRONIUS, MUTINY LEADER and SOLDIER #1 to #3 are standing at attention as CATO and LUCUIS enter.

***

CATO

Where are these sons of war that turn their backs on the foe and show defiance to their general?

SEMPRONIUS
(aside)

Curse on their souls, they stand amazed!

CATO

Treacherous men! Will you dishonor your past exploits and sully all your wars? Do you confess that is was not a zeal for Rome, nor love of liberty, that drew you this far, but the hope to share in the spoils of conquered towns? With such motives you do well to join with Cato's foes, and follow Caesar's banners. Why did I escape the serpent's venom to see this day! Behold, ungrateful men! Behold my bosom naked to your swords, let the man that's injured strike the first blow. Which of you suspects believes he is wronged, or thinks he suffers greater ills than Cato? Am I distinguished from you but by toils, superior toils, and a heavier weight of cares!

SEMPRONIUS
(aside, to himself)

By heavens they droop! All is lost.

CATO

Have you forgotten Libya's burning waste, its barren rocks, and hills of sand, its tainted air, and all its broods of poison?

SEMPRONIUS
(chiming in as if on CATO's side)

And if some scanty source of water appeared, when you scooped it up and offered it to Cato, did he not refuse until all others had drank? Didn't he lead you through the mid-day sun, and clouds of dust?

CATO

Worthless men! Go complain to Caesar. You could not survive the toils of war, nor bear the hardships that your leader endured.

LUCIUS

See, Cato, the unhappy men weep! Remorse, and sorrow for their crime appear in every look, and they plead for mercy.

CATO

Learn to be honest men, give up your leaders, and pardon shall descend on you.

SEMPRONIUS

Cato, commit these wretches to my care. First let them each be broken on the rack, then, with what life remains, impaled, and left to thrash about a bloody stake. The partners of their crimes will learn obedience, when they look up and see their fellow traitors stuck on a fork, and blackening in the sun.

LUCIUS

Sempronius, why, why would you press for such a fate for these wretched men?

SEMPRONIUS

(to LUCIUS)

How would you stop a rebellion?

(to CATO)

Lucius pities the poor offenders that would stain their hands with your blood!

CATO

Restrain yourself, Sempronius! See they suffer death, but remember they are men; do not make their tortures grievous.

(to LUCIUS)

Lucius, this degenerate age requires severity, and justice in its rigor. When by just vengeance guilty mortals perish, the gods behold their punishment with pleasure.

SEMPRONIUS

Cato, I execute your will with pleasure.

CATO

Meanwhile we'll sacrifice to liberty. Remember, my friends, the laws, the rights, and the plan of power were delivered down, from age to age, by your renowned forefathers, with the price of much blood. Let it never perish in your hands! But transmit it to your children.

(looking up towards sky)

Liberty, inspire our souls, and make our lives happy, or our deaths glorious in your just defense.

(exit CATO and LUCIUS)

ACT III, Scene 3

Setting: Open Air Square.

Cast: SEMPRONIUS, MUTINY LEADER, SOLDIER #1 to #3

At Rise: MUTINY LEADER addresses SEMPRONIUS, which becomes heated.   SOLDIER #1 to #3 are standing at attention observing.

***

MUTINY LEADER

Sempronius, you acted like yourself. One might think you were half earnest.

SEMPRONIUS

Villain, stand off! Groveling, worthless wretches, mongrels, poor faint-hearted traitors!

MUTINY LEADER

Now you carry it too far, Sempronius. Throw off your mask, we are all friends here.

SEMPRONIUS

Friends? When meager slaves mix in treason, they're thrown to the side if the plot succeeds. And if it fails, they're sure to die like dogs, as you shall do.

(enter GUARD)

SEMPRONIUS
(to GUARD)

Here, take these monsters, take them to their death.

MUTINY LEADER

So, it comes to this —

SEMPRONIUS
(to GUARD)

Quickly, but first pluck out their tongues, so they cannot sow sedition with their dying breath.

(ALL exit, except SEMPRONIUS)

ACT III, Scene 4

Setting: Open Air Square.

Cast: SYPHAX, SEMPRONIUS

At Rise: SEMPRONIUS is pacing angrily when SYPHAX enters.

***

SYPHAX

Our first plan was fruitless, my friend, but there still remains an after-game to play. My troops are mounted. The Numidian steeds snuff up the wind, and long to scour the desert, with you at our head. We'll force the gate where Marcus keeps his guard, and cut down all that would oppose our passage. A day's ride will bring us into Caesar's camp.

SEMPRONIUS

Confusion! I have failed half of my purpose. Marcia, the charming Marcia is left behind!

SYPHAX

Would you be a slave to a woman?

SEMPRONIUS

Syphax, I long to hold that proud maid and bend her stubborn virtue to my own passion. When I have done this, I'd cast her off!

SYPHAX

Well said! That's sounds like yourself, Sempronius. What hinders you? Find her and carry her away by your manly force!

SEMPRONIUS

But how can I gain entrance? Access is given to no one but Juba, and her brothers.

SYPHAX

You will have Juba's dress, and Juba's guards. The doors will open when Numidia's prince appears before the slaves that watch her.

SEMPRONIUS

Heavens, what a thought! Marcia will be my own!
How my bosom will swell with joy, when I behold her struggling in my arms. As Pluto seized Proserpine, and

conveyed the frightened maid to hell's gloom, so will I have Marcia!

(exeunt SEMPRONIUS and SYPHAX)

ACT III, Scene 5

Setting: Lucia's apartment with door.

Cast: LUCIA, MARCIA

At Rise: LUCIA and MARCIA in apartment having a serious/somber conversation.

***

LUCIA

Now tell me, Marcia, tell me from your soul, do you believe it is possible for a woman to suffer greater sorrows than I suffer?

MARCIA

Oh Lucia! Lucia! My heart also swells with griefs and sorrows. I could keep pace with your woes, tear for tear.

LUCIA

I know, you are doomed to be loved by Juba and your father's friend, Sempronius. But which of them has power to charm like Portius!

MARCIA

Must I still beg you not to name Sempronius? I don't like that loud boisterous man. Juba has the bravery of a hero and the softest of loves. He might make any woman happy – but not me.

LUCIA

And why not you? Come, do not hide your thoughts from one who knows a heart in love too well.

MARCIA

While Cato lives, his daughter has no right to love or hate, but to do only as he directs.

LUCIA

But what if your father gives you to Sempronius?

MARCIA

I dare not think of it, but if he should — Why are you adding to all the griefs I suffer? I hear the sound of feet! They march this way! When love pleas admission to our hearts, the woman that deliberates is lost.

(BOTH move away from door, huddling)

ACT III, Scene 6

Setting: Other side of door to Lucia's apartment

Cast: LUCIA, MARCIA, SEMPRONIUS, JUBA, GUARD

At Rise: SEMPRONIUS, dressed like JUBA, with GUARD. LUCIA and MARCIA are in apartment.

***

SEMPRONIUS
(aside)

My prey is trapped. I've tracked her to her den! (to GUARD) Be sure you mind my word, and when I give it, rush in at once, and seize upon the woman. Let not her cries distract you. (aside) How the young Numidian will wail to find his mistress lost! If anything could gladden my soul more, it would be to torture that barbarian.

(pause)

— But, listen, what is that?! Death to my hopes! It's him, it's Juba himself! There is only one way left — He must be murdered!

(enter JUBA)

JUBA

(out loud, from a distance)

What do I see? Who's this that dare assume my guards and wear the dress of Numidia's prince?

SEMPRONIUS

One that was born to shrink your arrogance!

JUBA

What is the meaning of this, Sempronius?!

SEMPRONIUS

My sword shall answer you!

JUBA

No, beware of mine, dreadful man!

(JUBA stabs SEMPRONIUS and SEMPRONIUS falls to the ground holding his wound. SEMPRONIUS's guard surrenders.)

SEMPRONIUS

Curse on my stars! Am I doomed to fall by a boy's hand?

In this vile Numidian dress, and for a worthless woman?
Oh for a peal of thunder that would make Earth, and Cato
tremble! Gods, this is the close of my life!

(SEMPRONIUS dies)

JUBA

With what a spring his furious soul broke loose, and left
his limbs still quivering on the ground!

(to GUARD)

And you two, come with me to Cato, so we may unravel
this mystery of fate.

(exit JUBA, and GUARD leaving SEMPRONIUS's
corpse)

ACT III, Scene 7

Setting: Lucia's apartment with door.

Cast: LUCIA, MARCIA, SEMPRONIUS, JUBA

At Rise: LUCIA and MARCIA are huddled together.

***

LUCIA

I'm sure that was the clash of swords! My troubled heart
is so cast down; it throbs with fear.

MARCIA
(looking at bottom of door)

See, Lucia, see! Here's blood! Here's blood and murder!

(opens door)

A Numidian! Heavens preserve the prince. But wait, the
face lies muffled within the garment.

(pulls back clothing)

Death to my sight! a crown, and purple robes! Oh gods! It's him, it's him! Juba, the loveliest youth that ever warmed a virgin's heart lies dead before us!

LUCIA

Now, Marcia, call upon your firmness of mind. You cannot put yourself through another trial.

MARCIA

Don't you believe I have cause for grief in my heart?

LUCIA

What can I say to give you comfort?

MARCIA

Do not talk of comfort, that is for lighter ills. Behold a sight that strikes all comfort dead.

(enter JUBA listening, aside)

MARCIA

I will indulge my sorrows, and give way to all the fury of despair. That man, that best of men, deserved it from me.

JUBA

(aside)

What do I hear? Was the turncoat Sempronius the best of men? Had I fallen like him, and been mourned like this

I'd be happy!

LUCIA

Here will I stand as a companion in your woes, and help you with my tears. When I behold a loss like yours, I forget half my own.

MARCIA

This empty world, to me a joyless desert, has nothing left to make poor Marcia happy.

JUBA
(aside)

I'm on the rack! Was he so near to her heart?

MARCIA

He was made up of love and charms, whatever a maid could wish for, or man admire. A delight to every eye! When he talked, the proudest Roman blushed to hear his virtues, and old age grew wise.

JUBA
(aside)

I shall run mad!

MARCIA

Oh Juba! Juba! Why do I think on what was! He's dead, and will never know how much I loved him!

JUBA

Where am I?! Am I what Marcia thinks?!

MARCIA

(bending over to the body)

The dear remains of the most loved of men! Neither modesty nor virtue forbid a last embrace, while thus —

JUBA

(JUBA runs up to MARCIA)

See, Marcia, see. The happy Juba lives! I live to catch your dear embrace, and to return it with eagerness of love.

MARCIA

Surely this is a dream! Dead and alive at once! If you are Juba, who lies there?

JUBA

A wretch, disguised like me on a cursed mission. Your father will know all about it. I could not bear to leave you in this neighborhood of death, so I flew, in all the haste of love, to find you. I must confess, that when I found you weeping, I was full of joy to see your tears.

MARCIA

The love that laid half smothered in my heart has broken through, and burns in its full luster. I can no longer conceal it from you.

JUBA

This, this is life indeed! Life worth preserving, such life I have never felt until now!

MARCIA

Believe me, prince, before I thought you were dead, I did not know myself how much I loved you.

JUBA

A fortunate mistake!

MARCIA

Lucia, your arm, let me rest upon it! The blood, that had left my heart, returns again in such joyous tides, it overcomes me. Lead to my apartment. — Oh prince! I blush to think what I have said, but fate has snatched the confession from me.

JUBA

I am so contented, I fear this is all a dream. Fortune, you have now made amends for all your past unkindness. Let Caesar have the world, if Marcia's mine!

(exeunt ALL)

ACT III, Scene 8

Setting: A large open hall in the Governor's Palace of Utica.

Cast: CATO, LUCIUS, PORTIUS, JUBA, MARCUS

At Rise: The sound of troops marching heard at a distance.

***

LUCIUS

I stand astonished! what, the bold Sempronius! The one who broke through the crowd of patriots, like a hurricane full of zeal?

CATO

Trust me, Lucius, our civil discords have produced such crimes, such monstrous crimes. I am surprised at nothing. (pause) Lucius, I am sick of this bad world! The daylight and the sun grow painful to me.

(pause)

But see Portius comes!

(enter PORTIUS)

CATO

(to PORTIUS)

What is this haste? Why are your looks so changed?

PORTIUS

Cato, My heart is grieved. I bring bad news.

CATO

Has Caesar shed more Roman blood?

PORTIUS

No, not so. The traitor Syphax was exercising his troops within the square, but when a signal was given he flew off on his horse to the south gate, where Marcus holds the watch. I called to stop him, but he just tossed his arm, and told me, he would not stay and perish like Sempronius.

CATO

Treacherous men! Hurry, my son, go see that your brother Marcus acts the Roman's part.

(exit PORTIUS)

CATO

Lucius, justice has given way to force. The conquered world is Caesar's, and I have no business in it any longer.

LUCIUS

While oppression, and injustice reign, the world will still demand her Cato's presence. In pity to mankind, submit to Caesar, and reconcile your mighty soul to life.

CATO

Would you have me live to increase the number of Caesar's slaves? Give up the cause of Rome, and submit to a tyrant?

LUCIUS

Caesar would never impose such ungenerous terms on Cato. Even his enemies confess the virtues of his humanity.

CATO

A curse on his virtues! He's undone his country, our country. Such popular humanity is treason! Observe the young Juba! He appears full of the guilt of his disloyal subjects.

LUCIUS

Alas! poor prince! His fate deserves compassion.

(enter JUBA)

JUBA

I blush, and am confounded to appear before your presence, Cato.

CATO

What's your crime?

JUBA

I'm a Numidian.

CATO

And a brave one too. You have a Roman soul.

JUBA

Have you not heard of my false countrymen?

CATO

My young prince, falsehood and fraud shoot up in every soil, the product of all climates — Rome has its Caesar.

JUBA

It is generous for you to comfort my distress.

CATO

It is just to give applause where it is deserved. Your virtue has stood the test of fortune, like the purest gold, tortured in the furnace, comes out more bright, and brings forth all its weight.

JUBA

My ravished heart overflows with joy. I'd rather gain your

praise, Cato, than Numidia's empire!

(re-enter PORTIUS)

PORTIUS

Grief on grief! My brother Marcus —

CATO

— What has he done? Did he forsake his post? Has he given way?

PORTIUS

Nothing of kind, my father. When I left to visit him, as you asked, I was met my soldiers, carrying Marcus on their shields. He was breathless and pale, and covered over with wounds. At the head of his few faithful friends, he withstood the shock of a whole host of foes -until he fell.

CATO

He was truly my son.

PORTIUS

But he did not fall until his sword had pierced through the false heart of Syphax. I saw the traitor shudder with the pangs of death, and bite the ground.

CATO

Thanks to the gods! My boy has done his duty. Portius, when I am dead, be sure to place his urn near mine.

PORTIUS

Long may they be together!

LUCIUS

Cato, gather your strength; the corpse of your dead son approaches! The citizens and senators have gathered around it, and attend to it with tears in their eyes.

CATO

(meeting the corpse)

Welcome, my son! (to the people carrying him) Here, lay him down, my friends, that I may view his bloody corpse, and count those glorious wounds. (pause) How beautiful is death when earned by virtue! What a pity is it that we can die but once to serve our country!

(looking up to the people)

Why look so sad, my friends?

(to PORTIUS)

Portius, behold your brother, and remember your life is not your own when Rome demands it!

JUBA

(aside)

When was there ever man a like this!

CATO

My friends, why do you morn? Do not let my loss afflict your hearts. It's Rome that needs our tears! The seat of the empire, the nurse of heroes, the delight of the gods, the one that humbled the proud tyrants of the earth, and set the nations free, Rome, it is no more. Oh liberty! Oh virtue! Oh my country!

JUBA

(aside)

Behold this upright man! He cries for Rome, not over his own dead son.

CATO

Whatever the Roman virtue has subdued, the sun's whole course, the day and year, are Caesar's. The great clans have fallen, her generals have been conquered - even Pompey fights for Caesar now! Oh my friends! This is the toil of fate, the work of ages, the Roman empire fallen! Oh cursed ambition! Our great forefathers had left him nothing to conquer but his own country.

JUBA

While Cato lives, Caesar will blush to see mankind enslaved, and be ashamed of his empire.

LUCIUS

Cato, it is time for you to save yourself and us.

CATO

Do not lose not a thought on me. Caesar will never say "I conquered Cato!" But it's your safety that fills my heart with anxious thoughts. A thousand secret terrors rise

in my soul; how shall I save my friends! It's only now,
Caesar, that I begin to fear you!

LUCIUS

Caesar will have mercy, if we ask it of him.

CATO

Then ask for it, I beg you! Let him know whatever was
done against him, was done by Cato. Add, if you wish,
that I request mercy for you from him. The virtue of my
friends should pass unpunished.

(to JUBA)

Juba, my heart is troubled for your sake. Should I advise
you to regain Numidia, or yield to the conqueror?

JUBA

May heaven abandon me, if I forsake you while I have life
in me.

CATO

Your virtues, prince, will one day make you great at
Rome. It will be no crime to have been Cato's friend.

(to PORTIUS)

Portius, draw near, my son, you have often seen your
father engaged in a corrupted state, battling with vice
and faction, and now you see me overpowered, desperate
for success. Let me advise you to retreat to the fields
of our home, where the great magistrate toiled with his

own hands, and all our frugal ancestors were blessed in humble virtues and a rural life. There live retired; pray for the peace of Rome. When vice prevails, and immoral men rule, the post of honor is a private station.

PORTIUS

I hope my father does not recommend a life to me that he scorns himself.

CATO

Farewell, my friends! If there be any of you who dare not trust the victor's clemency, know, there are ships prepared by my command, their sails already opening to the winds, they will carry you to your wished-for port. The conqueror draws near. Once more farewell!

(exit ALL, except CATO)

ACT III, Scene 9

Setting: Cato's private room

Cast: CATO

At Rise: CATO sitting by himself in a absorbed in thought, holding a scroll of Plato's Immortality of the Soul. A sword sits on the table next to him.

***

CATO

It must be so; Plato, you reason well! From where does this fond desire, this longing after immortality come? Or from where does this secret dread, this inward horror, of falling into naught begin? Why does the soul shrink back on itself when faced with destruction? Is it the divinity that stirs within us? Is it heaven itself, that points out a hereafter, and makes eternity known to man? Eternity?

a pleasing and dreadful thought! This wide, unbounded prospect, lies before me; but shadows, and darkness rest upon it. Here will I hold. If there's a power above us, he must delight in virtue. This world was made for Caesar. I'm weary of conjectures. This will end them.

(laying his hand on his sword)
My death and life, my bane and antidote are both before me. This moment brings me to my end; but it informs me I shall never die. The soul, secured in its existence, smiles at the drawn dagger, and defies its point. The stars shall fade away, the sun himself grows dim with age, and nature sink in years. But you will flourish in immortal youth, unhurt amidst the wrecks of matter, and the crush of worlds. Why does this heaviness hang upon me? This exhaustion that creeps through all my senses? Nature oppressed, and harassed out with care, sinks down to rest. This once I'll favor her, that my awakened soul may take her flight, renewed in all her strength, and fresh with life, an offering fit for heaven. Let guilt or fear disturb man's rest. Cato knows neither of them, indifferent in his choice to sleep or die.

ACT III, Scene 10

Setting: Cato's private room

Cast: CATO, PORTIUS

At Rise: CATO sitting and reading when PORTIUS enters.

***

CATO

But, how's this, my son? Were not my orders to be in private? Why am I disobeyed?

PORTIUS

I was troubled, father. What does this sword mean? This instrument of death? Let me take it from here!

CATO

I forbid it, rash youth!

PORTIUS

Please father, let the prayers of your friends, their tears, their common danger, take this from you.

CATO

Would you betray me? Would you give me up to be a slave in Caesar's hands? Leave me; learn obedience to a father!

PORTIUS

You know I'd rather die than disobey you.

CATO

As you should! I am the master of myself. Now, Caesar, let your troops storm our gates, and occupy each street, but Cato will open a passage for himself to mock your hopes!

PORTIUS

Please forgive your son; my grief hangs heavy on me! How can I be sure this is not the last time I will ever call you father? Do not be angry with me while I weep. My heart begs you to quit the dreadful purpose of your soul!

CATO

You have always been a good and dutiful son.

(CATO walks over and embraces PORTIUS)
Don't cry, my son; everything will be well again. The righteous gods, that I have sought to please, will assist Cato, and preserve his children.

PORTIUS

Your words give comfort to my drooping heart.

CATO

Portius, you may rely upon my conduct. Your father will not do anything that does not become him. Go now, my son, and see if there is anything you can do for your father's friends; go, see them off. My soul is quite weighed down with care, and needs the refreshment of a moment's sleep.

PORTIUS

My thoughts are more at ease, my heart revives.

(exit PORTIUS)

ACT III, Scene 11

Setting: A large open hall in the Governor's Palace of Utica.

Cast: PORTIUS, MARCIA, LUCIA, LUCIUS, JUBA, CATO

At Rise: PORTIUS and MARCIA are speaking aside from where LUCIA, LUCIUS and JUBA are.

***

PORTIUS
(aside, speaking privately to Marcia)
Oh Marcia, my sister, there is still hope! Our father will not cast away a life so needful to us, and to his country. He sent me with orders, that come from a mind at peace, and concerned for the safety of his friends. Marcia, take care that no one disturbs his slumber.

MARCIA

May the immortal powers that guard the just watch over
his couch, and calm his soul with easy dreams.

(looking up)
Remember all his virtues and show mankind that
goodness is your care!

(LUCIA walks over to where MARCIA is)

LUCIA

Where is your father, Marcia, where is Cato?

MARCIA

Lucia, speak low, he is resting. I feel a gentle hope rising
in my soul. We will be happy yet.

LUCIA

I tremble when I think of Cato. He is as stern, and awful
as a god. He does not know how to excuse human frailty,
or pardon weakness, because he has never felt it!

MARCIA

Though he has been awful to the foes of Rome, he is all
goodness, Lucia, always gentle to his friends. Filled with
domestic tenderness, the kindest father! I have always
found him easy to my wishes.

LUCIA

It is by his consent alone that we can be blessed. Marcia,

we both are involved in the same intricate distress,
the cruel hand of fate, that has destroyed your brother
Marcus, whom we both grieve for.

MARCIA

And we will grieve forever!

LUCIA

Our concern must be for Cato now.

MARCIA

Yes, let Cato live and commit the rest to heaven!

(enter LUCIUS)

LUCIUS

Sweet are the slumbers of the virtuous man! Oh Marcia,
I have seen your godlike father. Some invisible power
supports his soul, and bears it up in all its greatness. A
kind, refreshing sleep has fallen upon him. I saw him at
ease, lost in pleasing dreams. As I drew near his couch,
he smiled, and said, "Caesar, you cannot hurt me now."

MARCIA

Heavens, his mind still labors with some dreadful
thoughts.

LUCIUS

Lucia, why all this grief, these floods of sorrow? Dry up
your tears, my child, we all are safe while Cato lives; his

presence protects us.

(enter JUBA)

JUBA

Lucius, the horsemen are returned from viewing the number of our foes. They are now camped within a short hour's march! On the high point of the western tower we can see the setting sun play on their polished helmets; it covers all the field with gleams of fire.

LUCIUS

Marcia, it is time we should wake your father. Caesar is still disposed to give us terms, and waits at distance until he hears from Cato.

(enter PORTIUS)

LUCIUS

Portius, your looks speak somewhat of importance. What tidings do you bring? I think I see an unusual gladness in your eyes.

PORTIUS

As I was hurrying to the port, a ship arrived from Pompey's son! He journeyed through the realms of Spain and they call out for vengeance on his father's death; the whole nation is up in arms. If Cato were at their head, once more Rome might assert her rights, and claim her liberty -

(CATO groans from off stage)

PORTIUS

But hark! what means that groan! Oh give me way, and let me fly into my father's presence.

(exit PORTIUS)

LUCIUS

Cato, even while he slumbers, thinks of Rome, and in the wild disorder of his soul, mourns over his country.

(a second groan is heard from offstage)
Ah! a second groan! Heaven guard us all!

MARCIA

That is not the voice of one who sleeps! It is agonizing pain, there is death in that sound!

(re-enter PORTIUS)

PORTIUS

Marcia, what we feared has come to pass. Cato has fallen on his sword!

LUCIUS

Oh Portius, hide the horrors of your mournful tale, and let us guess the rest.

PORTIUS

I've raised him up, and placed him in his chair, where
pale, and faint, he gasps for breath, and, as his life
flows from him, demands to see his friends. His servants,
weeping, are bringing him here.

(CATO is brought onstage, carried in a chair)

MARCIA

Heaven help me pay the last sad duties to my father.

JUBA

Caesar, these are your triumphs, your exploits!

LUCIUS

Now is Rome fallen indeed!

CATO

(CATO brought forward in his chair; everyone gathers
around)

Here, set me down. Portius come near me. Have my
friends boarded the ships? Can you think of anything else
they may require? While I live, let me not live in vain.

(CATO is having trouble speaking)

Lucius, are you here? Oh, you are, good! Let our
friendship live between our children. Make Portius
happy with your daughter Lucia. Poor man, he weeps for
her.

(gathering his strength)

Marcia, my daughter, bend me forward. Juba loves you, Marcia. while Rome survived, a senator would not match his daughter with a king, but Caesar's arms have thrown down all those distinctions. Whoever is brave and virtuous, is a Roman. I am near to death. When will I get loose from this world of guilt and sorrow! And yet I think a beam of light breaks on my departing soul. I fear I've been too hasty. Oh, the powers, that search the heart of man, and weigh his innermost thoughts, if I have done wrong, please pardon me! The best of men make errors, but you are good — oh!

(CATO dies)

LUCIUS

There fled the greatest soul that ever warmed a Roman breast; Oh Cato, my friend! You will be religiously observed. (pause) Let us bring this corpse to Caesar, and lay it in his sight, that it may stand a fence between us and the victor's wrath. Cato, though dead, can still protect his friends. From here on, let contending nations know what dire effects flow from civil discord. This is what shakes our country with alarms, and makes Rome a prey to Roman arms, produces fraud, cruelty, and strife, and robs the guilty world of Cato's life.

Original Five Act Play

CATO; A Tragedy,

IN FIVE ACTS,

BY JOSEPH ADDISON, ESQ.

AS PERFORMED AT THE THEATRE ROYAL,
COVENT GARDEN.

PRINTED UNDER THE AUTHORITY OF THE
MANAGERS FROM THE PROMPT BOOK.

WITH REMARKS BY MRS. INCHBALD.

PARIS,

PRINTED FOR BAUDRY, ENGLISH, ITALIAN,
SPANISH, PORTUGUESE AND GERMAN

LIBRARY, RUE DU COQ-SAINT-HONORÉ.

1823.

Dramatis Personae

Cato,   Mr. Cooke.

Portius,   Mr. Siddons.

Marcus,   Mr. H. Johnston.

Sempronius,   Mr. Cory.

Juba,   Mr. Brunton.

Syphax,   Mr. Murray.

Lucius,   Mr. Claremont.

Decius,   Mr. Williams.

Lucia,   Miss Marriott.

Marcia,   Mrs. Litchfield.

Mutineers, Guards, etc._

SCENE--The Governor's Palace in Utica.

ACT THE FIRST

SCENE I.

A Hall.

***

[_Enter_ PORTIUS _and_ MARCUS.]

Por. The dawn is overcast, the morning low'rs, And heavily in clouds brings on the day, The great, the important day, big with the fate Of Cato and of Rome----Our father's death Would fill up all the guilt of civil war, And close the scene of blood. Already Cæsar Has ravaged more than half the globe, and sees Mankind grown thin by his destructive sword: Should he go farther, numbers would be wanting To form new battles, and support his crimes. Ye gods, what havoc does ambition make Among your works!

Marc. Thy steady temper, Portius, Can look on guilt, rebellion, fraud, and Cæsar, In the calm lights of mild philosophy; I'm tortured e'en to madness, when I think On the proud victor--ev'ry time he's named, Pharsalia rises to my view!--I see Th' insulting tyrant, prancing o'er the field, Strew'd with Rome's citizens, and drench'd in slaughter; His horse's hoofs wet with patrician blood! Oh, Portius! is there not some chosen curse, Some hidden thunder in the stores of Heav'n, Red with uncommon wrath, to blast the man Who owes his greatness to his country's ruin?

Por. Believe me, Marcus, 'tis an impious greatness, And mix'd with too much horror to be envied: How does the lustre of our father's actions, Through the dark cloud of ills that cover him, Break out, and burn with more triumphant brightness! His sufferings shine, and spread a glory round him; Greatly unfortunate, he fights the cause Of honour, virtue, liberty, and Rome. His sword ne'er fell, but on the guilty head; Oppression, tyranny, and pow'r usurp'd, Draw all the vengeance of his arm upon them.

Marc. Who knows not this? but what can Cato do Against a world, a base, degenerate world, That courts the yoke, and bows the neck to Cæsar? Pent up in Utica, he vainly forms A poor epitome of Roman greatness, And, cover'd with Numidian guards, directs A feeble army, and an empty senate, Remnants of mighty battles fought in vain. By Heav'n, such virtue, join'd with such success, Distracts my very soul! Our father's fortune Would almost tempt us to renounce his precepts.

Por. Remember what our father oft has told us: The ways of Heav'n are dark and intricate, Puzzled in mazes, and perplex'd with errors; Our understanding traces them in vain, Lost and bewilder'd in the fruitless search; Nor sees with how much art the windings run, Nor where the regular confusion ends.

Marc. These are suggestions of a mind at ease:-- Oh, Portius! didst thou taste but half the griefs That wring my soul, thou couldst not talk thus coldly. Passion unpitied, and successless love, Plant daggers in my heart, and aggravate My other griefs.--Were but my Lucia kind----

Por. Thou see'st not that thy brother is thy rival; But I must hide it, for I know thy temper.

[_Aside._]

Behold young Juba, the Numidian prince, With how much care he forms himself to glory, And breaks the fierceness of his native temper, To copy out our father's bright example. He loves our sister Marcia, greatly loves her; His eyes, his looks, his actions, all betray it; But still the smother'd fondness burns within him; When most it swells, and labours for a vent, The sense of honour, and desire of fame, Drive the big passion back into his heart.

What! shall an African, shall Juba's heir, Reproach great Cato's son, and show the world A virtue wanting in a Roman soul?

Marc. Portius, no more! your words leave stings behind them. Whene'er did Juba, or did Portius, show A virtue that has cast me at a distance, And thrown me out in the pursuits of honour?

Por. Marcus, I know thy gen'rous temper well; Fling but the appearance of dishonour on it, It straight takes fire, and mounts into a blaze.

Marc. A brother's suff'rings claim a brother's pity.

Por. Heav'n knows, I pity thee----Behold my eyes, Ev'n whilst I speak--Do they not swim in tears? Were but my heart as naked to thy view, Marcus would see it bleed in his behalf. _Marc._ Why then dost treat me with rebukes, instead Of kind condoling cares, and friendly sorrow?

Por. Oh, Marcus! did I know the way to ease Thy troubled heart, and mitigate thy pains, Marcus, believe me, I could die to do it.

Marc. Thou best of brothers, and thou best of friends! Pardon a weak distemper'd soul, that swells With sudden gusts, and sinks as soon in calms, The sport of passions. But Sempronius comes: He must not find this softness hanging on me.

[_Exit_ MARCUS.]

[_Enter_ SEMPRONIUS.]

Sem. Conspiracies no sooner should be form'd Than executed. What means Portius here? I like not that cold youth. I must dissemble, And speak a language foreign to my heart.

[_Aside._]

Good-morrow, Portius; let us once embrace, Once more embrace, while yet we both are free. To-morrow, should we thus express our friendship, Each might receive a slave into his arms; This sun, perhaps, this morning sun's the last That e'er shall rise on Roman liberty.

Por. My father has this morning call'd together To this poor hall, his little Roman senate, (The leavings of Pharsalia) to consult If he can yet oppose the mighty torrent That bears down Rome and all her gods before it, Or must at length give up the world to Cæsar.

Sem. Not all the pomp and majesty of Rome Can raise her senate more than Cato's presence. His virtues render our assembly awful, They strike with something like religious fear, And make even Cæsar tremble at the head Of armies flush'd with conquest. Oh, my Portius! Could I but call that wond'rous man my father, Would but thy sister Marcia be propitious To thy friend's vows, I might be blest indeed!

Por. Alas, Sempronius! wouldst thou talk of love
To Marcia, whilst her father's life's in danger? Thou
might'st as well court the pale, trembling vestal, When
she beholds the holy flame expiring.

Sem. The more I see the wonders of thy race, The more
I'm charm'd. Thou must take heed, my Portius; The world
has all its eyes on Cato's son; Thy father's merit sets thee
up to view, And shows thee in the fairest point of light,
To make thy virtues or thy faults conspicuous.

Por. Well dost thou seem to check my ling'ring here
In this important hour--I'll straight away, And while the
fathers of the senate meet In close debate, to weigh th'
events of war, I'll animate the soldiers' drooping courage
With love of freedom and contempt of life; I'll thunder in
their ears their country's cause, And try to rouse up all
that's Roman in them. 'Tis not in mortals to command
success, But we'll do more, Sempronius--we'll deserve
it.

[_Exit._]

Sem. Curse on the stripling! how he apes his sire!
Ambitiously sententious--But I wonder Old Syphax
comes not; his Numidian genius Is well disposed to
mischief, were he prompt And eager on it; but he must be
spurr'd, And every moment quicken'd to the course. Cato

has used me ill; he has refused His daughter Marcia to my
ardent vows. Besides, his baffled arms, and ruin'd cause,
Are bars to my ambition. Cæsar's favour, That show'rs
down greatness on his friends, will raise me To Rome's
first honours. If I give up Cato, I claim, in my reward, his
captive daughter. But Syphax comes---

[_Enter_ SYPHAX.]

Syph. Sempronius, all is ready; I've sounded my
Numidians, man by man, And find them ripe for a revolt:
they all Complain aloud of Cato's discipline, And wait
but the command to change their master.

Sem. Believe me, Syphax, there's no time to waste; Ev'n
while we speak, our conqueror comes on, And gathers
ground upon us every moment. Alas! thou know'st not
Cæsar's active soul, With what a dreadful course he
rushes on From war to war. In vain has nature form'd
Mountains and oceans t'oppose his passage; He bounds
o'er all. One day more Will set the victor thund'ring at
our gates. But, tell me, hast thou yet drawn o'er young
Juba? That still would recommend thee more to Cæsar,
And challenge better terms.

Syph. Alas! he's lost! He's lost, Sempronius; all his
thoughts are full Of Cato's virtues--But I'll try once
more (For every instant I expect him here) If yet I can
subdue those stubborn principles Of faith and honour,

and I know not what, That have corrupted his Numidian temper, And struck th' infection into all his soul.

Sem. Be sure to press upon him every motive. Juba's surrender, since his father's death, Would give up Afric into Cæsar's hands, And make him lord of half the burning zone.

Syph. But is it true, Sempronius, that your senate Is call'd together? Gods! thou must be cautious; Cato has piercing eyes, and will discern Our frauds, unless they're cover'd thick with art.

Sem. Let me alone, good Syphax, I'll conceal My thoughts in passion ('tis the surest way); I'll bellow out for Rome, and for my country, And mouth at Cæsar, till I shake the senate. Your cold hypocrisy's a stale device, A worn-out trick: wouldst thou be thought in earnest, Clothe thy feign'd zeal in rage, in fire, in fury!

Syph. In troth, thou'rt able to instruct grey hairs, And teach the wily African deceit.

Sem. Once more be sure to try thy skill on Juba. Remember, Syphax, we must work in haste; Oh, think what anxious moments pass between The birth of plots, and their last fatal periods! Oh, 'tis a dreadful interval of time, Fill'd up with horror all, and big with death! Destruction hangs on every word we speak, On every thought, till the concluding stroke Determines all, and closes our design.

[_Exit._]

Syph. I'll try if yet I can reduce to reason This headstrong youth, and make him spurn at Cato. The time is short; Cæsar comes rushing on us-- But hold! young Juba sees me, and approaches!

[_Enter_ JUBA.]

Jub. Syphax, I joy to meet thee thus alone. I have observed of late thy looks are fall'n, O'ercast with gloomy cares and discontent; Then tell me, Syphax, I conjure thee, tell me, What are the thoughts that knit thy brow in frowns, And turn thine eye thus coldly on thy prince?

Syph. 'Tis not my talent to conceal my thoughts, Or carry smiles and sunshine in my face, When discontent sits heavy at my heart; I have not yet so much the Roman in me.

Jub. Why dost thou cast out such ungenerous terms Against the lords and sov'reigns of the world? Dost thou not see mankind fall down before them, And own the force of their superior virtue? Is there a nation in the wilds of Africa, Amidst our barren rocks and burning sands, That does not tremble at the Roman name?

Syph. Gods! where's the worth that sets these people up Above your own Numidia's tawny sons? Do they with tougher sinews bend the bow? Or flies the javelin swifter to its mark, Launch'd from the vigour of a Roman arm? Who like our active African instructs The fiery steed, and trains him to his hand? Or guides in troops th' embattled elephant Laden with war? These, these are arts, my prince, In which your Zama does not stoop to Rome.

Jub. These all are virtues of a meaner rank: Perfections that are placed in bones and nerves. A Roman soul is bent on higher views; Turn up thy eyes to Cato; There may'st thou see to what a godlike height The Roman virtues lift up mortal man. While good, and just, and anxious for his friends, He's still severely bent against himself; And when his fortune sets before him all The pomps and pleasures that his soul can wish, His rigid virtue will accept of none.

Syph. Believe me, prince, there's not an African That traverses our vast Numidian deserts In quest of prey, and lives upon his bow, But better practises those boasted virtues. Coarse are his meals, the fortune of the chase; Amidst the running stream he slakes his thirst; Toils all the day, and, at the approach of night, On the first friendly bank he throws him down, Or rests his head upon a rock till morn; Then rises fresh, pursues his wonted game, And if the following day he chance to find A new repast, or an untasted spring, Blesses his stars, and thinks it luxury.

Jub. Thy prejudices, Syphax, won't discern What virtues grow from ignorance and choice, Nor how the hero differs from the brute. Where shall we find the man that bears affliction, Great and majestic in his griefs, like Cato? How does he rise against a load of woes, And thank the gods that threw the weight upon him!

Syph. 'Tis pride, rank pride, and haughtiness of soul; I think the Romans call it stoicism. Had not your royal father thought so highly Of Roman virtue, and of Cato's cause, He had not fall'n by a slave's hand inglorious.

Jub. Why dost thou call my sorrows up afresh? My father's name brings tears into my eyes.

Syph. Oh, that you'd profit by your father's ills!

Jub. What wouldst thou have me do?

Syph. Abandon Cato.

Jub. Syphax, I should be more than twice an orphan By such a loss.

Syph. Ay, there's the tie that binds you! You long to call him father. Marcia's charms Work in your heart unseen, and plead for Cato. No wonder you are deaf to all I say.

Jub. Syphax, your zeal becomes importunate; I've hitherto permitted it to rave, And talk at large; but learn to keep it in, Lest it should take more freedom than I'll give it.

Syph. Sir, your great father never used me thus. Alas, he's dead! but can you e'er forget The tender sorrows, And repeated blessings, Which you drew from him in your last farewell? The good old king, at parting, wrung my hand, (His eyes brimful of tears) then sighing cried, Pr'ythee be careful of my son!----His grief Swell'd up so high, he could not utter more.

Jub. Alas! thy story melts away my soul! That best of fathers! how shall I discharge The gratitude and duty that I owe him?

Syph. By laying up his counsels in your heart.

Jub. His counsels bade me yield to thy direction: Then, Syphax, chide me in severest terms, Vent all thy passion, and I'll stand its shock, Calm and unruffled as a summer sea, When not a breath of wind flies o'er its surface.

Syph. Alas! my prince, I'd guide you to your safety.

Jub. I do believe thou wouldst; but tell me how?

Syph. Fly from the fate that follows Cæsar's foes.

Jub. My father scorn'd to do it.

Syph. And therefore died.

Jub. Better to die ten thousand thousand deaths, Than

wound my honour.

Syph. Rather say, your love.

Jub. Syphax, I've promised to preserve my temper; Why wilt thou urge me to confess a flame I long have stifled, and would fain conceal?

Syph. Believe me, prince, though hard to conquer love, 'Tis easy to divert and break its force. Absence might cure it, or a second mistress Light up another flame, and put out this. The glowing dames of Zama's royal court Have faces flush'd with more exalted charms; Were you with these, my prince, you'd soon forget The pale, unripen'd beauties of the north.

Jub. 'Tis not a set of features, or complexion, The tincture of a skin, that I admire: Beauty soon grows familiar to the lover, Fades in his eye, and palls upon the sense. The virtuous Marcia tow'rs above her sex: True, she is fair (Oh, how divinely fair!), But still the lovely maid improves her charms, With inward greatness, unaffected wisdom, And sanctity of manners; Cato's soul Shines out in every thing she acts or speaks, While winning mildness and attractive smiles Dwell in her looks, and, with becoming grace, Soften the rigour of her father's virtue.

Syph. How does your tongue grow wanton in her praise! But on my knees, I beg you would consider--

Jub. Ha! Syphax, is't not she?--She moves this way; And with her Lucia, Lucius's fair daughter. My heart beats thick--I pr'ythee, Syphax, leave me.

Syph. Ten thousand curses fasten on them both! Now will the woman, with a single glance, Undo what I've been lab'ring all this while.

[_Exit_ SYPHAX.]

[_Enter_ MARCIA _and_ LUCIA.]

Jub. Hail, charming maid! How does thy beauty smooth The face of war, and make even horror smile! At sight of thee my heart shakes off its sorrows; I feel a dawn of joy break in upon me, And for a while forget th' approach of Cæsar.

Marcia. I should be grieved, young prince, to think my presence Unbent your thoughts, and slacken'd them to arms, While, warm with slaughter, our victorious foe Threatens aloud, and calls you to the field.

Jub. Oh, Marcia, let me hope thy kind concerns And gentle wishes follow me to battle! The thought will give new vigour to my arm, And strength and weight to my descending sword, And drive it in a tempest on the foe.

Marcia. My pray'rs and wishes always shall attend The friends of Rome, the glorious cause of virtue, And men approved of by the gods and Cato.

Jub. That Juba may deserve thy pious cares, I'll gaze for ever on thy godlike father, Transplanting one by one, into my life, His bright perfections, till I shine like him.

Marcia. My father never, at a time like this, Would lay out his great soul in words, and waste Such precious moments.

Jub. Thy reproofs are just, Thou virtuous maid; I'll hasten to my troops, And fire their languid souls with Cato's virtue. If e'er I lead them to the field, when all The war shall stand ranged in its just array, And dreadful pomp, then will I think on thee; Oh, lovely maid! then will I think on thee; And, in the shock of charging hosts, remember What glorious deeds should grace the man who hopes For Marcia's love.

[_Exit_ JUBA.]

Lucia. Marcia, you're too severe; How could you chide the young good-natured prince, And drive him from you with so stern an air, A prince that loves, and dotes on you to death?

Marcia. 'Tis therefore, Lucia, that I chide him from me; His air, his voice, his looks, and honest soul, Speak all so movingly in his behalf, I dare not trust myself to hear him talk.

Lucia. Why will you fight against so sweet a passion,

And steel your heart to such a world of charms?

Marcia. How, Lucia! wouldst thou have me sink away In pleasing dreams, and lose myself in love, When ev'ry moment Cato's life's at stake? Cæsar comes arm'd with terror and revenge, And aims his thunder at my father's head. Should not the sad occasion swallow up My other cares?

Lucia. Why have I not this constancy of mind, Who have so many griefs to try its force? Sure, Nature form'd me of her softest mould, Enfeebled all my soul with tender passions, And sunk me ev'n below my own weak sex: Pity and love, by turns, oppress my heart.

Marcia. Lucia, disburden all thy cares on me, And let me share thy most retired distress. Tell me, who raises up this conflict in thee?

Lucia. I need not blush to name them, when I tell thee They're Marcia's brothers, and the sons of Cato.

Marcia. They both behold thee with their sister's eyes, And often have reveal'd their passion to me. But tell me, which of them is Lucia's choice?

Lucia. Suppose 'twere Portius, could you blame my choice?-- Oh, Portius, thou hast stolen away my soul! Marcus is over warm, his fond complaints Have so much earnestness and passion in them, I hear him with a secret kind of horror, And tremble at his vehemence of temper.

Marcia. Alas, poor youth! How will thy coldness raise Tempests and storms in his afflicted bosom! I dread the consequence.

Lucia. You seem to plead Against your brother Portius.

Marcia. Heav'n forbid. Had Portius been the unsuccessful lover, The same compassion would have fall'n on him.

Lucia. Was ever virgin love distress'd like mine! Portius himself oft falls in tears before me As if he mourn'd his rival's ill success; Then bids me hide the motions of my heart, Nor show which way it turns--so much he fears The sad effect that it will have on Marcus.

Marcia. Let us not, Lucia, aggravate our sorrows, But to the gods submit the event of things. Our lives, discolour'd with our present woes, May still grow bright, and smile with happier hours. So the pure limpid stream, when foul with stains Of rushing torrents and descending rains, Works itself clear, and, as it runs, refines, Till, by degrees, the floating mirror shines; Reflects each flower that on the border grows, And a new heav'n in its fair bosom shows.

[_Exeunt._]

ACT THE SECOND

SCENE I.

The Senate sitting.

Flourish.

***

[_Enter_ CATO.]

Cato. Fathers, we once again are met in council;
Cæsar's approach has summon'd us together, And Rome
attends her fate from our resolves. How shall we treat
this bold aspiring man? Success still follows him, and
backs his crimes; Pharsalia gave him Rome, Egypt has
since Received his yoke, and the whole Nile is Cæsar's.
Why should I mention Juba's overthrow, And Scipio's
death? Numidia's burning sands Still smoke with blood.

'Tis time we should decree What course to take. Our foe
advances on us, And envies us even Lybia's sultry deserts.
Fathers, pronounce your thoughts: are they still fix'd To
hold it out, and fight it to the last? Or are your hearts
subdued at length, and wrought, By time and ill success,
to a submission? Sempronius, speak.

Sem. Gods! can a Roman senate long debate Which of
the two to chuse, slav'ry or death! No; let us rise at once,
gird on our swords, And, at the head of our remaining
troops, Attack the foe, break through the thick array
Of his throng'd legions, and charge home upon him.
Perhaps some arm, more lucky than the rest, May reach
his heart, and free the world from bondage. Rise, fathers,
rise! 'tis Rome demands your help; Rise, and revenge
her slaughter'd citizens, Or share their fate!-- To battle!
Great Pompey's shade complains that we are slow; And
Scipio's ghost walks unrevenged amongst us.

Cato. Let not a torrent of impetuous zeal Transport
thee thus beyond the bounds of reason; True fortitude
is seen in great exploits, That justice warrants, and
that wisdom guides; All else is tow'ring phrensy and
distraction. Lucius, we next would know what's your
opinion.

Luc. My thoughts, I must confess, are turn'd on peace.
Already have our quarrels fill'd the world With widows,
and with orphans: Scythia mourns Our guilty wars, and

earth's remotest regions Lie half unpeopled by the feuds of Rome: 'Tis time to sheathe the sword, and spare mankind. Already have we shown our love to Rome, Now let us show submission to the gods. We took up arms, not to revenge ourselves, But free the commonwealth; when this end fails, Arms have no further use. Our country's cause, That drew our swords, now wrests them from our hands. And bids us not delight in Roman blood, Unprofitably shed. What men could do, Is done already: Heav'n and earth will witness, If Rome must fall, that we are innocent.

Cato. Let us appear nor rash nor diffident; Immod'rate valour swells into a fault; And fear, admitted into public councils, Betrays like treason. Let us shun them both. Fathers, I cannot see that our affairs Are grown thus desp'rate: we have bulwarks round us; Within our walls are troops inured to toil In Afric's heat, and season'd to the sun; Numidia's spacious kingdom lies behind us, Ready to rise at its young prince's call. While there is hope, do not distrust the gods; But wait, at least, till Cæsar's near approach Force us to yield. 'Twill never be too late To sue for chains, and own a conqueror. Why should Rome fall a moment ere her time? No, let us draw her term of freedom out In its full length, and spin it to the last, So shall we gain still one day's liberty; And let me perish, but in Cato's judgment, A day, an hour, of virtuous liberty, Is worth a whole eternity in bondage.

[_Enter_ MARCUS.]

Marc. Fathers, this moment, as I watch'd the gate,
Lodged on my post, a herald is arrived From Cæsar's
camp, and with him comes old Decius, The Roman
knight; he carries in his looks Impatience, and demands
to speak with Cato.

Cato. By your permission, fathers--bid him enter.

[_Exit_ MARCUS.]

Decius was once my friend, but other prospects Have
loosed those ties, and bound him fast to Cæsar. His
message may determine our resolves.

[_Enter_ DECIUS.]

Dec. Cæsar sends health to Cato--

Cato. Could he send it To Cato's slaughter'd friends,
it would be welcome. Are not your orders to address the
senate?

Dec. My business is with Cato. Cæsar sees The straits
to which you're driven; and, as he knows Cato's high
worth, is anxious for your life.

Cato. My life is grafted on the fate of Rome. Would he
save Cato, bid him spare his country. Tell your dictator
this; and tell him, Cato Disdains a life which he has
power to offer.

Dec. Rome and her senators submit to Cæsar; Her gen'rals and her consuls are no more, Who check'd his conquests, and denied his triumphs. Why will not Cato be this Cæsar's friend?

Cato. These very reasons thou hast urged forbid it.

Dec. Cato, I've orders to expostulate And reason with you, as from friend to friend: Think on the storm that gathers o'er your head, And threatens ev'ry hour to burst upon it; Still may you stand high in your country's honours-- Do but comply, and make your peace with Cæsar; Rome will rejoice, and cast its eyes on Cato, As on the second of mankind.

Cato. No more; I must not think of life on such conditions.

Dec. Cæsar is well acquainted with your virtues, And therefore sets this value on your life. Let him but know the price of Cato's friendship, And name your terms.

Cato. Bid him disband his legions, Restore the commonwealth to liberty, Submit his actions to the public censure, And stand the judgment of a Roman senate. Bid him do this, and Cato is his friend.

Dec. Cato, the world talks loudly of your wisdom----

Cato. Nay, more, though Cato's voice was ne'er employ'd To clear the guilty, and to varnish crimes,

Myself will mount the rostrum in his favour, And strive to gain his pardon from the people.

Dec. A style like this becomes a conqueror.

Cato. Decius, a style like this becomes a Roman.

Dec. What is a Roman, that is Cæsar's foe?

Cato. Greater than Cæsar: he's a friend to virtue.

Dec. Consider, Cato, you're in Utica, And at the head of your own little senate: You do not thunder in the capitol, With all the mouths of Rome to second you.

Cato. Let him consider that, who drives us hither. 'Tis Cæsar's sword has made Rome's senate little, And thinn'd its ranks. Alas! thy dazzled eye Beholds this man in a false glaring light, Which conquest and success have thrown upon him; Did'st thou but view him right, thou'dst see him black With murder, treason, sacrilege, and crimes That strike my soul with horror but to name them. I know thou look'st on me as on a wretch Beset with ills, and cover'd with misfortunes; But, by the gods I swear, millions of worlds Should never buy me to be like that Cæsar.

Dec. Does Cato send this answer back to Cæsar, For all his gen'rous cares and proffer'd friendship?

Cato. His cares for me are insolent and vain:

Presumptuous man! the gods take care of Cato. Would Cæsar show the greatness of his soul, Bid him employ his care for these my friends, And make good use of his ill-gotten pow'r, By sheltering men much better than himself.

Dec. Your high, unconquer'd heart makes you forget You are a man. You rush on your destruction. But I have done. When I relate hereafter The tale of this unhappy embassy, All Rome will be in tears.

[_Exit_ DECIUS.]

Sem. Cato, we thank thee. The mighty genius of immortal Rome Speaks in thy voice; thy soul breathes liberty. Cæsar will shrink to hear the words thou utter'st, And shudder in the midst of all his conquests.

Luc. The senate owns its gratitude to Cato, Who with so great a soul consults its safety, And guards our lives, while he neglects his own.

Sem. Sempronius gives no thanks on this account. Lucius seems fond of life; but what is life? 'Tis not to stalk about, and draw fresh air From time to time, or gaze upon the sun; 'Tis to be free. When liberty is gone, Life grows insipid.

Cato. Come; no more, Sempronius; All here are friends to Rome, and to each other. Let us not weaken still the weaker side By our divisions.

Sem. Cato, my resentments Are sacrificed to Rome--I stand reproved.

Cato. Fathers, 'tis time you come to a resolve.

Luc. Cato, we all go in to your opinion; Cæsar's behaviour has convinced the senate We ought to hold it out till terms arrive.

Sem. We ought to hold it out till death; but, Cato, My private voice is drown'd amidst the senate's.

Cato. Then let us rise, my friends, and strive to fill This little interval, this pause of life (While yet our liberty and fates are doubtful) With resolution, friendship, Roman bravery, And all the virtues we can crowd into it; That Heav'n may say, it ought to be prolong'd. Fathers, farewell--The young Numidian prince Comes forward, and expects to know our counsels.

[_Exeunt_ SENATORS.]

[_Enter_ JUBA.]

Juba, the Roman senate has resolved, Till time give better prospects, still to keep The sword unsheathed, and turn its edge on Cæsar.

Jub. The resolution fits a Roman senate. But, Cato, lend me for a while thy patience, And condescend to hear a young man speak. My father, when, some days before his death, He order'd me to march for Utica, (Alas! I thought not then his death so near!) Wept o'er me, press'd me in his aged arms, And, as his griefs gave way, "My son," said he, "Whatever fortune shall befal thy father, Be Cato's friend; he'll train thee up to great And virtuous deeds; do but observe him well, Thou'lt shun misfortunes, or thou'lt learn to bear them."

Cato. Juba, thy father was a worthy prince, And merited, alas! a better fate; But Heav'n thought otherwise.

Jub. My father's fate, In spite of all the fortitude that shines Before my face, in Cato's great example, Subdues my soul, and fills my eyes with tears.

Cato. It is an honest sorrow, and becomes thee.

Jub. My father drew respect from foreign climes: The kings of Afric sought him for their friend; Kings far remote, that rule, as fame reports, Behind the hidden sources of the Nile, In distant worlds, on t'other side the sun; Oft have their black ambassadors appear'd, Loaden with gifts, and fill'd the courts of Zama.

Cato. I am no stranger to thy father's greatness.

Jub. I would not boast the greatness of my father, But point out new alliances to Cato. Had we not better leave this Utica, To arm Numidia in our cause, and court Th' assistance of my father's powerful friends? Did they know Cato, our remotest kings Would pour embattled multitudes about him: Their swarthy hosts would darken all our plains, Doubling the native horror of the war, And making death more grim.

Cato. And canst thou think Cato will fly before the sword of Cæsar? Reduced, like Hannibal, to seek relief From court to court, and wander up and down A vagabond in Africa?

Jub. Cato, perhaps I'm too officious; but my forward cares Would fain preserve a life of so much value. My heart is wounded, when I see such virtue Afflicted by the weight of such misfortunes.

Cato. Thy nobleness of soul obliges me. But know, young prince, that valour soars above What the world calls misfortune and affliction. These are not ills; else would they never fall On Heav'n's first fav'rites, and the best of men. The gods, in bounty, work up storms about us, That give mankind occasion to exert Their hidden strength, and throw out into practice Virtues, which shun the day, and lie conceal'd In the smooth seasons and the calms of life.

Jub. I'm charm'd, whene'er thou talk'st; I pant for virtue, And all my soul endeavours at perfection.

Cato. Dost thou love watchings, abstinence, and toil, Laborious virtues all? Learn them from Cato; Success and fortune must thou learn from Cæsar.

Jub. The best good fortune that can fall on Juba, The whole success at which my heart aspires, Depends on Cato.

Cato. What does Juba say? Thy words confound me.

Jub. I would fain retract them. Give them me back again: they aimed at nothing.

Cato. Tell me thy wish, young prince; make not my ear A stranger to thy thoughts.

Jub. Oh! they're extravagant; Still let me hide them.

Cato. What can Juba ask, That Cato will refuse?

Jub. I fear to name it. Marcia--inherits all her father's virtues.

Cato. What wouldst thou say?

Jub. Cato, thou hast a daughter.

Cato. Adieu, young prince; I would not hear a word Should lessen thee in my esteem. Remember, The hand of fate is over us, and Heav'n Exacts severity from all our thoughts. It is not now a time to talk of aught But chains or conquest, liberty or death.

[_Exit._]

[_Enter_ SYPHAX.]

Syph. How's this, my prince? What, cover'd with confusion? You look as if yon stern philosopher Had just now chid you.

Jub. Syphax, I'm undone!

Syph. I know it well.

Jub. Cato thinks meanly of me.

Syph. And so will all mankind.

Jub. I've open'd to him The weakness of my soul--my love for Marcia.

Syph. Cato's a proper person to intrust A love-tale with!

Jub. Oh, I could pierce my heart, My foolish heart!

Syph. Alas, my prince, how are you changed of late! I've known young Juba rise before the sun, To beat the thicket where the tiger slept, Or seek the lion in his dreadful haunts. I've seen you, Ev'n in the Lybian dog-days, hunt him down, Then charge him close, And, stooping from your horse, Rivet the panting savage to the ground.

Jub. Pr'ythee, no more.

Syph. How would the old king smile, To see you weigh the paws, when tipp'd with gold, And throw the shaggy spoils about your shoulders!

Jub. Syphax, this old man's talk, though honey flow'd In ev'ry word, would now lose all its sweetness. Cato's displeased, and Marcia lost for ever.

Syph. Young prince, I yet could give you good advice; Marcia might still be yours.

Jub. As how, dear Syphax?

Syph. Juba commands Numidia's hardy troops, Mounted on steeds unused to the restraint Of curbs or bits, and fleeter than the winds: Give but the word, we snatch this damsel up, And bear her off.

Jub. Can such dishonest thoughts Rise up in man? Wouldst thou seduce my youth To do an act that would destroy mine honour?

Syph. Gods, I could tear my hair to hear you talk! Honour's a fine imaginary notion, That draws in raw and inexperienced men To real mischiefs, while they hunt a shadow.

Jub. Wouldst thou degrade thy prince into a ruffian?

Syph. The boasted ancestors of these great men, Whose virtues you admire, were all such ruffians. This dread of nations, this almighty Rome, That comprehends in her wide empire's bounds All under Heav'n, was founded on a rape; Your Scipios, Cæsars, Pompeys, and your Catos (The gods on earth), are all the spurious blood Of violated maids, of ravish'd Sabines. _Jub._ Syphax, I fear that hoary head of thine Abounds too much in our Numidian wiles.

Syph. Indeed, my prince, you want to know the world.

Jub. If knowledge of the world makes men perfidious, May Juba ever live in ignorance!

Syph. Go, go; you're young.

Jub. Gods, must I tamely bear This arrogance, unanswer'd! Thou'rt a traitor, A false old traitor.

Syph. I've gone too far.

[_Aside._]

Jub. Cato shall know the baseness of thy soul.

Syph. I must appease this storm, or perish in it.

[_Aside._]

Young prince, behold these locks, that are grown white Beneath a helmet in your father's battles.

Jub. Those locks shall ne'er protect thy insolence.

Syph. Must one rash word, the infirmity of age, Throw down the merit of my better years? This the reward of a whole life of service!-- Curse on the boy! how steadily he hears me!

[_Aside._]

Jub. Syphax, no more! I would not hear you talk.

Syph. Not hear me talk! what, when my faith to Juba, My royal master's son, is call'd in question? My prince may strike me dead, and I'll be dumb; But whilst I live I must not hold my tongue, And languish out old age in his displeasure.

Jub. Thou know'st the way too well into my heart. I do believe thee loyal to thy prince.

Syph. What greater instance can I give? I've offer'd To do an action which my soul abhors, And gain you whom you love, at any price.

Jub. Was this thy motive? I have been too hasty.

Syph. And 'tis for this my prince has call'd me traitor.

Jub. Sure thou mistakest; I did not call thee so.

Syph. You did, indeed, my prince, you call'd me traitor. Nay, further, threatened you'd complain to Cato. Of what, my prince, would you complain to Cato? That Syphax loves you, and would sacrifice His life, nay, more, his honour, in your service?

Jub. Syphax, I know thou lovest me; but indeed Thy zeal for Juba carried thee too far. Honour's a sacred tie, the law of kings, The noble mind's distinguishing perfection, That aids and strengthens Virtue where it meets her, And imitates her actions where she is not; It ought not to be sported with.

Syph. Believe me, prince, you make old Syphax weep To hear you talk--but 'tis with tears of joy. If e'er your father's crown adorn your brows, Numidia will be blest by Cato's lectures.

Jub. Syphax, thy hand; we'll mutually forget The warmth of youth, and forwardness of age: Thy prince esteems thy worth, and loves thy person. If e'er the sceptre come into my hand, Syphax shall stand the second in my kingdom.

Syph. Why will you overwhelm my age with kindness? My joys grow burdensome, I sha'n't support it.

Jub. Syphax, farewell. I'll hence, and try to find Some blest occasion, that may set me right In Cato's thoughts. I'd rather have that man Approve my deeds, than worlds for my admirers.

[_Exit._]

Syph. Young men soon give, and soon forget, affronts;

Old age is slow in both--A false old traitor! These words, rash boy, may chance to cost thee dear. My heart had still some foolish fondness for thee; But hence, 'tis gone! I give it to the winds: Cæsar, I'm wholly thine.

[_Enter_ SEMPRONIUS.]

All hail, Sempronius! Well, Cato's senate is resolved to wait The fury of a siege, before it yields.

Sem. Syphax, we both were on the verge of fate; Lucius declared for peace, and terms were offer'd To Cato, by a messenger from Cæsar. Should they submit, ere our designs are ripe, We both must perish in the common wreck, Lost in the general, undistinguish'd ruin.

Syph. But how stands Cato?

Sem. Thou hast seen mount Atlas: Whilst storms and tempests thunder on its brows, And oceans break their billows at its feet, It stands unmoved, and glories in its height; Such is that haughty man; his tow'ring soul, 'Midst all the shocks and injuries of fortune, Rises superior, and looks down on Cæsar.

Syph. But what's this messenger?

Sem. I've practised with him, And found a means to let the victor know That Syphax and Sempronius are his friends. But let me now examine in my turn; Is Juba fix'd?

Syph. Yes--but it is to Cato. I've tried the force of every reason on him, Soothed and caress'd; been angry, soothed again; Laid safety, life, and interest in his sight; But all are vain, he scorns them all for Cato.

Sem. Come, 'tis no matter; we shall do without him. He'll make a pretty figure in a triumph, And serve to trip before the victor's chariot. Syphax, I now may hope thou hast forsook Thy Juba's cause, and wishest Marcia mine.

Syph. May she be thine as fast as thou wouldst have her.

Sem. Syphax, I love that woman; though I curse Her and myself, yet, spite of me, I love her.

Syph. Make Cato sure, and give up Utica, Cæsar will ne'er refuse thee such a trifle. But are thy troops prepared for a revolt? Does the sedition catch from man to man, And run among the ranks?

Sem. All, all is ready; The factious leaders are our friends, that spread Murmurs and discontents among the soldiers; They count their toilsome marches, long fatigues, Unusual fastings, and will hear no more This medley of philosophy and war. Within an hour they'll storm the senate house.

Syph. Meanwhile I'll draw up my Numidian troops Within the square, to exercise their arms, And, as I see occasion, favour thee. I laugh, to see how your unshaken Cato Will look aghast, while unforeseen destruction Pours in upon him thus from every side. So, where our wide Numidian wastes extend, Sudden th' impetuous hurricanes descend, Wheel through the air, in circling eddies play, Tear up the sands, and sweep whole plains away. The helpless traveller, with wild surprise, Sees the dry desert all around him rise, And, smother'd in the dusty whirlwind, dies.

[_Exeunt._]

ACT THE THIRD

SCENE I.

A Chamber.

***

[_Enter_ MARCUS _and_ PORTIUS.]

Marc. Thanks to my stars, I have not ranged about The wilds of life, ere I could find a friend; Nature first pointed out my Portius to me, And early taught me, by her secret force, To love thy person, ere I knew thy merit, Till what was instinct, grew up into friendship.

Por. Marcus, the friendships of the world are oft Confed'racies in vice, or leagues of pleasure; Ours has severest virtue for its basis, And such a friendship ends not but with life.

Marc. Portius, thou know'st my soul in all its weakness; Then, pr'ythee, spare me on its tender side; Indulge me but in love, my other passions Shall rise and fall by virtue's nicest rules.

Por. When love's well-timed, 'tis not a fault to love. The strong, the brave, the virtuous, and the wise, Sink in the soft captivity together.

Marc. Alas, thou talk'st like one that never felt Th' impatient throbs and longings of a soul, That pants and reaches after distant good! A lover does not live by vulgar time; Believe me, Portius, in my Lucia's absence Life hangs upon me, and becomes a burden; And yet, when I behold the charming maid, I'm ten times more undone; while hope and fear, And grief and rage, and love, rise up at once, And with variety of pain distract me.

Por. What can thy Portius do to give thee help?

Marc. Portius, thou oft enjoy'st the fair one's presence; Then undertake my cause, and plead it to her With all the strength and heat of eloquence Fraternal love and friendship can inspire. Tell her thy brother languishes to death, And fades away, and withers in his bloom; That he forgets his sleep, and loathes his food; That youth, and health, and war, are joyless to him; Describe his anxious days, and restless nights, And all the torments that thou see'st me suffer.

Por. Marcus, I beg thee give me not an office, That suits with me so ill. Thou know'st my temper.

Marc. Wilt thou behold me sinking in my woes, And wilt thou not reach out a friendly arm, To raise me from amidst this plunge of sorrows?

Por. Marcus, thou canst not ask what I'd refuse; But here, believe me, I've a thousand reasons----

Marc. I know thou'lt say my passion's out of season, That Cato's great example and misfortunes Should both conspire to drive it from my thoughts. But what's all this to one that loves like me? O Portius, Portius, from my soul I wish Thou did'st but know thyself what 'tis to love! Then wouldst thou pity and assist thy brother.

Por. What should I do? If I disclose my passion, Our friendship's at an end: if I conceal it, The world will call me false to a friend and brother.

[_Aside._]

Marc. But see, where Lucia, at her wonted hour, Amid the cool of yon high marble arch, Enjoys the noon-day breeze! Observe her, Portius; That face, that shape, those eyes, that heav'n of beauty! Observe her well, and blame me if thou canst.

Por. She sees us, and advances----

Marc. I'll withdraw, And leave you for a while. Remember, Portius, Thy brother's life depends upon thy tongue.

[_Exit._]

[_Enter_ LUCIA.]

Lucia. Did not I see your brother Marcus here? Why did he fly the place, and shun my presence?

Por. Oh, Lucia, language is too faint to show His rage of love; it preys upon his life; He pines, he sickens, he despairs, he dies!

Lucia. How wilt thou guard thy honour, in the shock Of love and friendship! Think betimes, my Portius, Think how the nuptial tie, that might ensure Our mutual bliss, would raise to such a height Thy brother's griefs, as might perhaps destroy him.

Por. Alas, poor youth! What dost thou think, my Lucia? His gen'rous, open, undesigning heart Has begg'd his rival to solicit for him! Then do not strike him dead with a denial.

Lucia. No, Portius, no; I see thy sister's tears, Thy father's anguish, and thy brother's death, In the pursuit of our ill-fated loves; And, Portius, here I swear, to Heav'n I swear, To Heav'n, and all the powers that judge mankind, Never to mix my plighted hands with thine, While such a cloud of mischief hangs upon us, But to forget our loves, and drive thee out From all my thoughts--as far as I am able.

Por. What hast thou said? I'm thunderstruck--recall Those hasty words, or I am lost for ever.

Lucia. Has not the vow already pass'd my lips? The gods have heard it, and 'tis seal'd in heav'n. May all the vengeance that was ever pour'd On perjured heads, o'erwhelm me if I break it!

Por. Fix'd in astonishment, I gaze upon thee, Like one just blasted by a stroke from heav'n, Who pants for breath and stiffens, yet alive, In dreadful looks, a monument of wrath!

Lucia. Think, Portius, think thou see'st thy dying brother Stabb'd at his heart, and all besmear'd with blood, Storming at Heav'n and thee! Thy awful sire Sternly demands the cause, the accursed cause, That robs him of his son: poor Marcia trembles, Then tears her hair, and, frantic in her griefs, Calls out on Lucia. What could Lucia answer, Or how stand up in such a scene of sorrow?

Por. To my confusion and eternal grief, I must approve the sentence that destroys me.

Lucia. Portius, no more; thy words shoot through my heart, Melt my resolves, and turn me all to love. Why are those tears of fondness in thy eyes? Why heaves thy heart? Why swells thy soul with sorrow? It softens me too much--Farewell, my Portius! Farewell, though death is in the word,--for ever!

Por. Stay, Lucia, stay! What dost thou say? For ever? Thou must not go; my soul still hovers o'er thee, And can't get loose.

Lucia. If the firm Portius shake, To hear of parting, think what Lucia suffers!

Por. 'Tis true, unruffled and serene, I've met The common accidents of life, but here Such an unlook'd-for storm of ills falls on me. It beats down all my strength--I cannot bear it. We must not part.

Lucia. What dost thou say? Not part! Hast thou forgot the vow that I have made? Are not there heavens, and gods, that thunder o'er us? --But see, thy brother Marcus bends this way; I sicken at the sight. Once more, farewell. Farewell, and know, thou wrong'st me, if thou think'st Ever was love or ever grief like mine.

[_Exit_ LUCIA.]

[_Enter_ MARCUS.]

Marc. Portius, what hopes? How stands she? am I doom'd To life or death?

Por. What wouldst thou have me say?

Marc. What means this pensive posture? Thou appear'st Like one amazed and terrified.

Por. I've reason.

Marc. Thy downcast looks, and thy disorder'd thoughts, Tell me my fate. I ask not the success My cause has found.

Por. I'm grieved I undertook it.

Marc. What, does the barbarous maid insult my heart, My aching heart, and triumph in my pains? That I could cast her from my thoughts for ever!

Por. Away! you're too suspicious in your griefs; Lucia, though sworn never to think of love, Compassionates your pains, and pities you.

Marc. Compassionates my pains, and pities me! What is compassion, when 'tis void of love? Fool that I was, to choose so cold a friend To urge my cause!--Compassionates my pains! Pr'ythee what art, what rhet'ric didst thou use To gain this mighty boon?--She pities me! To one that asks the warm returns of love, Compassion's cruelty, 'tis scorn, 'tis death--

Por. Marcus, no more; have I deserved this treatment?

Marc. What have I said? Oh! Portius, Oh, forgive me!

A soul exasperated in ills, falls out With every thing--its friend, itself--but hah!

[_Shout._]

What means that shout, big with the sounds of war? What new alarm?

Por. A second, louder yet, Swells in the wind, and comes more full upon us.

Marc. Oh, for some glorious cause to fall in battle! Lucia, thou hast undone me: thy disdain Has broke my heart; 'tis death must give me ease.

Por. Quick let us hence. Who knows if Cato's life Stands sure? Oh, Marcus, I am warm'd; my heart Leaps at the trumpet's voice, and burns for glory.

[_Exeunt._]

***

SCENE II.

Part of the Senate House.

Enter SEMPRONIUS, _with_ LEADERS _of the Mutiny_.

***

Sem. At length the winds are raised, the storm blows high! Be it your care, my friends, to keep it up In all its fury, and direct it right, Till it has spent itself on Cato's head. Meanwhile, I'll herd among his friends, and seem One of the number, that, whate'er arrive, My friends and fellow soldiers may be safe.

[_Exit._]

1 Lead. We are all safe; Sempronius is our friend. Sempronius is as brave a man as Cato. But, hark, he enters. Bear up boldly to him; Be sure you beat him down, and bind him fast; This day will end our toils. Fear nothing, for Sempronius is our friend.

[_Enter_ SEMPRONIUS, _with_ CATO, LUCIUS, PORTIUS, _and_ MARCUS.]

Cato. Where are those bold, intrepid sons of war, That greatly turn their backs upon the foe, And to their general send a brave defiance?

Sem. Curse on their dastard souls, they stand astonish'd!

[_Aside._]

Cato. Perfidious men! And will you thus dishonour

Your past exploits, and sully all your wars? Why could not Cato fall Without your guilt! Behold, ungrateful men, Behold my bosom naked to your swords, And let the man that's injured strike the blow. Which of you all suspects that he is wrong'd, Or thinks he suffers greater ills than Cato? Am I distinguished from you but by toils, Superior toils, and heavier weight of cares? Painful pre-eminence!

Sem. Confusion to the villains! all is lost!

[_Aside._]

Cato. Have you forgotten Lybia's burning waste, Its barren rocks, parch'd earth, and hills of sand, Its tainted air, and all its broods of poison? Who was the first to explore th' untrodden path, When life was hazarded in ev'ry step? Or, fainting in the long laborious march, When, on the banks of an unlook'd-for stream, You sunk the river with repeated draughts, Who was the last of all your host who thirsted?

Sem. Did not his temples glow In the same sultry winds and scorching heats?

Cato. Hence, worthless men! hence! and complain to Cæsar, You could not undergo the toil of war, Nor bear the hardships that your leader bore.

Lucius. See, Cato, see the unhappy men: they weep! Fear, and remorse, and sorrow for their crime, Appear in ev'ry look, and plead for mercy.

Cato. Learn to be honest men; give up yon leaders, And pardon shall descend on all the rest.

Sem. Cato, commit these wretches to my care; First let them each be broken on the rack, Then, with what life remains, impaled, and left To writhe at leisure round the bloody stake; There let them hang, and taint the southern wind. The partners of their crime will learn obedience.

Cato. Forbear, Sempronius!--see they suffer death, But in their deaths remember they are men; Strain not the laws, to make their tortures grievous. Lucius, the base, degen'rate age requires Severity. When by just vengeance guilty mortals perish, The gods behold the punishment with pleasure, And lay th' uplifted thunderbolt aside.

Sem. Cato, I execute thy will with pleasure.

Cato. Meanwhile, we'll sacrifice to liberty. Remember, O my friends! the laws, the rights, The gen'rous plan of power delivered down From age to age by your renown'd forefathers, (So dearly bought, the price of so much blood:) Oh, let it never perish in your hands! But piously transmit it to your children. Do thou, great liberty, inspire our souls, And make our lives in thy possession happy, Or our deaths glorious in thy just defence.

[_Exeunt_ CATO, _etc._]

1 Lead. Sempronius, you have acted like yourself. One would have thought you had been half in earnest.

Sem. Villain, stand off; base, grov'ling, worthless wretches, Mongrels in faction, poor faint-hearted traitors!

1 Lead. Nay, now, you carry it too far, Sempronius!

Sem. Know, villains, when such paltry slaves presume To mix in treason, if the plot succeeds, They're thrown neglected by; but if it fails, They're sure to die like dogs, as you shall do. Here, take these factious monsters, drag them forth To sudden death.

1 Lead. Nay, since it comes to this--

Sem. Dispatch them quick, but first pluck out their tongues, Lest with their dying breath they sow sedition.

[_Exeunt_ GUARDS, _with their_ LEADERS.]

[_Enter_ SYPHAX.]

Syph. Our first design, my friend, has proved abortive; Still there remains an after-game to play; My troops are mounted; Let but Sempronius head us in our flight, We'll force the gate where Marcus keeps his guard, And hew down all that would oppose our passage. A day will bring us into Cæsar's camp.

Sem. Confusion! I have fail'd of half my purpose:

Marcia, the charming Marcia's left behind!

Syph. How! will Sempronius turn a woman's slave?

Sem. Think not thy friend can ever feel the soft
Unmanly warmth and tenderness of love. Syphax, I long
to clasp that haughty maid, And bend her stubborn virtue
to my passion: When I have gone thus far, I'd cast her off.

Syph. Well said! that's spoken like thyself, Sempronius!
What hinders, then, but that thou find her out, And hurry
her away by manly force?

Sem. But how to gain admission? For access Is given to
none but Juba, and her brothers.

Syph. Thou shalt have Juba's dress, and Juba's guards;
The doors will open, when Numidia's prince Seems to
appear before the slaves that watch them.

Sem. Heavens, what a thought is there! Marcia's my
own! How will my bosom swell with anxious joy, When
I behold her struggling in my arms, With glowing
beauty, and disorder'd charms, While fear and anger,
with alternate grace, Pant in her breast, and vary in her
face! So Pluto seized off Proserpine, convey'd To hell's
tremendous gloom th' affrighted maid; There grimly
smiled, pleased with the beauteous prize, Nor envied Jove
his sunshine and his skies.

[_Exeunt._]

ACT THE FOURTH

SCENE I.

A Chamber.

***

[_Enter_ LUCIA _and_ MARCIA.]

Lucia. Now, tell me, Marcia, tell me from thy soul, If thou believest 'tis possible for woman To suffer greater ills than Lucia suffers?

Marcia Oh, Lucia, Lucia, might my big swol'n heart Vent all its griefs, and give a loose to sorrow, Marcia could answer thee in sighs, keep pace With all thy woes, and count out tear for tear.

Lucia. I know thou'rt doom'd alike to be beloved By Juba, and thy father's friend, Sempronius: But which of these has power to charm like Portius?

Marcia. Still, I must beg thee not to name Sempronius. Lucia, I like not that loud, boist'rous man. Juba, to all the bravery of a hero, Adds softest love, and more than female sweetness; Juba might make the proudest of our sex, Any of womankind, but Marcia, happy.

Lucia. And why not Marcia? Come, you strive in vain To hide your thoughts from one who knows too well The inward glowings of a heart in love.

Marcia. While Cato lives, his daughter has no right To love or hate, but as his choice directs.

Lucia. But should this father give you to Sempronius?

Marcia. I dare not think he will: but if he should-- Why wilt thou add to all the griefs I suffer, Imaginary ills, and fancied tortures? I hear the sound of feet! They march this way. Let us retire, and try if we can drown Each softer thought in sense of present danger: When love once pleads admission to our hearts, In spite of all the virtues we can boast, The woman that deliberates is lost.

[_Exeunt._]

[_Enter_ SEMPRONIUS, _dressed like_ JUBA, _with_ NUMIDIAN GUARDS.]

Sem. The deer is lodged, I've track'd her to her covert.
How will the young Numidian rave to see His mistress
lost! If aught could glad my soul, Beyond the enjoyment
of so bright a prize, 'Twould be to torture that young, gay
barbarian. --But, hark! what noise! Death to my hopes!
'tis he, 'Tis Juba's self! there is but one way left----

[_Enter_ JUBA.]

Jub. What do I see? Who's this that dares usurp The
guards and habits of Numidia's prince?

Sem. One that was born to scourge thy arrogance,
Presumptuous youth!

Jub. What can this mean? Sempronius!

Sem. My sword shall answer thee. Have at thy heart.

Jub. Nay then, beware thy own, proud, barbarous man.

[SEMPRONIUS _falls_.]

Sem. Curse on my stars! Am I then doom'd to fall By a
boy's hand, disfigured in a vile Numidian dress, and for
a worthless woman? Gods, I'm distracted! this my close
of life! Oh, for a peal of thunder, that would make Earth,
sea, and air, and heav'n, and Cato tremble!

[_Dies._]

Jub. I'll hence to Cato, That we may there at length

unravel all This dark design, this mystery of fate.

[_Exit_ JUBA.]

[_Enter_ LUCIA _and_ MARCIA.]

Lucia. Sure 'twas the clash of swords; my troubled heart Is so cast down, and sunk amidst its sorrows, It throbs with fear, and aches at ev'ry sound. Oh, Marcia, should thy brothers, for my sake-- I die away with horror at the thought!

Marcia. See, Lucia, see! here's blood! here's blood and murder! Ha! a Numidian! Heav'n preserve the prince! The face lies muffled up within the garment, But ah! death to my sight! a diadem, And royal robes! O gods! 'tis he, 'tis he! Juba lies dead before us!

Lucia. Now, Marcia, now, call up to thy assistance Thy wonted strength and constancy of mind; Thou canst not put it to a greater trial.

Marcia. Lucia, look there, and wonder at my patience; Have I not cause to rave, and beat my breast, To rend my heart with grief, and run distracted?

Lucia. What can I think, or say, to give thee comfort?

Marcia. Talk not of comfort, 'tis for lighter ills: Behold a sight that strikes all comfort dead.

[_Enter_ JUBA, _listening_.]

I will indulge my sorrows, and give way To all the pangs
and fury of despair; That man, that best of men, deserved
it from me.

Jub. What do I hear? and was the false Sempronius
That best of men? Oh, had I fall'n like him, And could
have been thus mourn'd, I had been happy.

Marcia. 'Tis not in fate to ease my tortured breast. Oh,
he was all made up of love and charms! Whatever maid
could wish, or man admire: Delight of every eye; when
he appear'd, A secret pleasure gladden'd all that saw him;
But when he talk'd, the proudest Roman blush'd To hear
his virtues, and old age grew wise. Oh, Juba! Juba!

Jub. What means that voice? Did she not call on Juba?

Marcia. Why do I think on what he was? he's dead! He's
dead, and never knew how much I loved him! Lucia, who
knows but his poor, bleeding heart, Amidst its agonies,
remember'd Marcia, And the last words he utter'd call'd
me cruel! Alas! he knew not, hapless youth, he knew not
Marcia's whole soul was full of love and Juba!

Jub. Where am I? Do I live? or am indeed What Marcia
thinks? All is Elysium round me!

Marcia. Ye dear remains of the most loved of men,
Nor modesty nor virtue here forbid A last embrace, while
thus----

Jub. See, Marcia, see,

[_Throwing himself before her._]

The happy Juba lives! he lives to catch That dear embrace, and to return it too, With mutual warmth, and eagerness of love.

Marcia. With pleasure and amaze I stand transported! If thou art Juba, who lies there?

Jub. A wretch, Disguised like Juba on a cursed design. I could not bear To leave thee in the neighbourhood of death, But flew, in all the haste of love, to find thee; I found thee weeping, and confess this once, Am rapt with joy, to see my Marcia's tears.

Marcia. I've been surprised in an unguarded hour, But must not go back; the love, that lay Half smother'd in my breast, has broke through all Its weak restraints, and burns in its full lustre. I cannot, if I would, conceal it from thee.

Jub. My joy, my best beloved, my only wish! How shall I speak the transport of my soul!

Marcia. Lucia, thy arm. Lead to my apartment. Oh! prince! I blush to think what I have said, But fate has wrested the confession from me; Go on, and prosper in the paths of honour. Thy virtue will excuse my passion for thee, And make the gods propitious to our love.

[_Exeunt_ MARCIA _and_ LUCIA.]

Jub. I am so blest, I fear 'tis all a dream. Fortune,
thou now hast made amends for all Thy past unkindness:
I absolve my stars. What though Numidia add her
conquer'd towns And provinces to swell the victor's
triumph, Juba will never at his fate repine: Let Cæsar
have the world, if Marcia's mine.

[_Exit._]

***

SCENE II.

The Street.

A March at a distance.

***

[_Enter_ CATO _and_ LUCIUS.]

Luc. I stand astonish'd! What, the bold Sempronius,
That still broke foremost through the crowd of patriots,

As with a hurricane of zeal transported, And virtuous even to madness--

Cato. Trust me, Lucius, Our civil discords have produced such crimes, Such monstrous crimes, I am surprized at nothing.

--Oh Lucius, I am sick of this bad world! The daylight and the sun grow painful to me.

[_Enter_ PORTIUS.]

But see, where Portius comes: what means this haste? Why are thy looks thus changed?

Por. My heart is grieved, I bring such news as will afflict my father.

Cato. Has Cæsar shed more Roman blood?

Por. Not so. The traitor Syphax, as within the square He exercised his troops, the signal given, Flew off at once with his Numidian horse To the south gate, where Marcus holds the watch; I saw, and call'd to stop him, but in vain: He toss'd his arm aloft, and proudly told me, He would not stay, and perish, like Sempronius.

Cato. Perfidious man! But haste, my son, and see Thy brother Marcus acts a Roman's part.

[_Exit_ PORTIUS.]

--Lucius, the torrent bears too hard upon me: Justice gives way to force: the conquer'd world Is Cæsar's! Cato has no business in it.

Luc. While pride, oppression, and injustice reign, The world will still demand her Cato's presence. In pity to mankind submit to Cæsar, And reconcile thy mighty soul to life.

Cato. Would Lucius have me live to swell the number Of Cæsar's slaves, or by a base submission Give up the cause of Rome, and own a tyrant?

Luc. The victor never will impose on Cato Ungen'rous terms. His enemies confess The virtues of humanity are Cæsar's.

Cato. Curse on his virtues! they've undone his country. Such popular humanity is treason---- But see young Juba; the good youth appears, Full of the guilt of his perfidious subjects!

Luc. Alas, poor prince! his fate deserves compassion.

[_Enter_ JUBA.]

Jub. I blush, and am confounded to appear Before thy presence, Cato.

Cato. What's thy crime?

Jub. I'm a Numidian.

Cato. And a brave one, too. Thou hast a Roman soul.

Jub. Hast thou not heard of my false countrymen?

Cato. Alas, young prince! Falsehood and fraud shoot up in ev'ry soil, The product of all climes--Rome has its Cæsars.

Jub. 'Tis generous thus to comfort the distress'd.

Cato. 'Tis just to give applause, where 'tis deserved: Thy virtue, prince, has stood the test of fortune, Like purest gold, that, tortured in the furnace, Comes out more bright, and brings forth all its weight.

Jub. What shall I answer thee? I'd rather gain Thy praise, O Cato! than Numidia's empire.

[_Enter_ PORTIUS.]

Por. Misfortune on misfortune! grief on grief! My brother Marcus----

Cato. Ha! what has he done? Has he forsook his post? Has he given way? Did he look tamely on, and let them pass?

Por. Scarce had I left my father, but I met him Borne on the shields of his surviving soldiers, Breathless and pale, and cover'd o'er with wounds. Long, at the head of his few faithful friends, He stood the shock of a whole host of foes, Till, obstinately brave, and bent on death,

Oppress'd with multitudes, he greatly fell.

Cato. I'm satisfied.

Por. Nor did he fall, before His sword had pierced thro' the false heart of Syphax. Yonder he lies. I saw the hoary traitor Grin in the pangs of death, and bite the ground.

Cato. Thanks to the gods, my boy has done his duty. --Portius, when I am dead, be sure you place His urn near mine.

Por. Long may they keep asunder!

Luc. Oh, Cato, arm thy soul with all its patience; See where the corpse of thy dead son approaches! The citizens and senators alarm'd, Have gather'd round it, and attend it weeping.

[CATO _meeting the Corpse_.--SENATORS _attending_.]

Cato. Welcome, my son! Here lay him down, my friends, Full in my sight, that I may view at leisure The bloody corse, and count those glorious wounds. --How beautiful is death, when earn'd by virtue! Who would not be that youth? What pity is it, That we can die but once, to serve our country! --Why sits this sadness on your brows, my friends? I should have blush'd, if Cato's house had stood Secure, and flourish'd in a civil war. Portius, behold thy brother, and remember, Thy life is not thy own when

Rome demands it.

Jub. Was ever man like this!

Cato. Alas, my friends, Why mourn you thus? let not a private loss Afflict your hearts. 'Tis Rome requires our tears, The mistress of the world, the seat of empire, The nurse of heroes, the delight of gods, That humbled the proud tyrants of the earth, And set the nations free; Rome is no more. Oh, liberty! Oh, virtue! Oh, my country!

Jub. Behold that upright man! Rome fills his eyes With tears, that flow'd not o'er his own dear son.

[_Aside._]

Cato. Whate'er the Roman virtue has subdued, The sun's whole course, the day and year, are Cæsar's: For him the self-devoted Decii died, The Fabii fell, and the great Scipios conquer'd: Ev'n Pompey fought for Cæsar. Oh, my friends, How is the toil of fate, the work of ages, The Roman empire, fall'n! Oh, cursed ambition! Fall'n into Cæsar's hands! Our great forefathers Had left him nought to conquer but his country.

Jub. While Cato lives, Cæsar will blush to see Mankind enslaved, and be ashamed of empire.

Cato. Cæsar ashamed! Has he not seen Pharsalia?

Luc. 'Tis time thou save thyself and us.

Cato. Lose not a thought on me; I'm out of danger:
Heaven will not leave me in the victor's hand. Cæsar shall
never say, he conquer'd Cato. But oh, my friends! your
safety fills my heart With anxious thoughts; a thousand
secret terrors Rise in my soul. How shall I save my
friends? 'Tis now, O Cæsar, I begin to fear thee!

Luc. Cæsar has mercy, if we ask it of him.

Cato. Then ask it, I conjure you; let him know,
Whate'er was done against him, Cato did it. Add, if
you please, that I request of him,-- That I myself, with
tears, request it of him,-- The virtue of my friends may
pass unpunish'd. Juba, my heart is troubled for thy sake.
Should I advise thee to regain Numidia, Or seek the
conqueror?

Jub. If I forsake thee Whilst I have life, may Heaven
abandon Juba!

Cato. Thy virtues, prince, if I foresee aright, Will one
day make thee great; at Rome, hereafter, 'Twill be no
crime to have been Cato's friend. Portius, draw near: my
son, thou oft hast seen Thy sire engaged in a corrupted
state, Wrestling with vice and faction: now thou see'st me
Spent, overpower'd, despairing of success. Let me advise
thee to retreat betimes To thy paternal seat, the Sabine
field; Where the great Censor toil'd with his own hands,
And all our frugal ancestors were bless'd In humble

virtues, and a rural life; There live retired, pray for the peace of Rome; Content thyself to be obscurely good. When vice prevails, and impious men bear sway, The post of honour is a private station.

Por. I hope my father does not recommend A life to Portius that he scorns himself.

Cato. Farewell, my friends! If there be any of you Who dare not trust the victor's clemency, Know there are ships prepared, by my command, That shall convey you to the wish'd-for port. Is there aught else, my friends, I can do for you? The conqueror draws near. Once more, farewell! If e'er we meet hereafter, we shall meet In happier climes, and on a safer shore, Where Cæsar never shall approach us more.

[_Pointing to his dead son._]

There, the brave youth, with love of virtue fired, Who greatly in his country's cause expired, Shall know he conquer'd. The firm patriot there, Who made the welfare of mankind his care, Though still by faction, vice, and fortune crost, Shall find the gen'rous labour was not lost.

[_Exeunt._]

ACT THE FIFTH

SCENE I.

A Chamber.

CATO _solus, sitting in a thoughtful Posture; in his Hand, Plato's Book on the Immortality of the Soul. A drawn Sword on the Table by him._

***

Cato. It must be so--Plato, thou reason'st well--Else whence this pleasing hope, this fond desire, This longing after immortality? Or whence this secret dread, and inward horror, Of falling into nought? Why shrinks the soul Back on herself, and startles at destruction? 'Tis the divinity that stirs within us; 'Tis Heav'n itself that points out an hereafter, And intimates eternity to man. Eternity! thou pleasing, dreadful thought! Through what variety of untried being, Through what new scenes and changes must we pass? The wide, the unbounded prospect lies before me; But shadows, clouds, and darkness, rest upon it. Here will I hold. If there's a Power above us (And that there is, all Nature cries aloud Through all her works), He must delight in virtue; And that which He delights in must be happy. But when, or where?--this world was made for Cæsar: I'm weary of conjectures--this must end them.

[_Laying his hand upon his sword._]

Thus am I doubly arm'd: my death and life, My bane and antidote, are both before me. This in a moment brings me to an end; But this informs me I shall never die. The soul, secured in her existence, smiles At the drawn dagger, and defies its point. The stars shall fade away, the sun himself Grow dim with age, and nature sink in years, But thou shalt flourish in immortal youth, Unhurt amidst the war of elements, The wreck of matter, and the crush of worlds. What means this heaviness, that hangs upon me? This lethargy, that creeps through all my senses? Nature, oppress'd and harass'd out with care, Sinks down to rest. This once I'll favour her, That my awaken'd soul may take her flight, Renew'd in all her strength, and fresh with life, An offering lit for Heav'n. Let guilt or fear Disturb man's rest, Cato knows neither of them, Indiff'rent in his choice to sleep or die.

[_Enter_ PORTIUS.]

But, hah! who's this? my son! Why this intrusion? Were not my orders that I would be private? Why am I disobey'd?

Por. Alas, my father! What means this sword, this instrument of death? Let me convey it hence.

Cato. Rash youth, forbear!

Por. Oh, let the pray'rs, th' entreaties of your friends, Their tears, their common danger, wrest it from you!

Cato. Wouldst thou betray me? Wouldst thou give me up, A slave, a captive, into Cæsar's hands? Retire, and learn obedience to a father, Or know, young man--

Por. Look not thus sternly on me; You know, I'd rather die than disobey you.

Cato. 'Tis well! again I'm master of myself. Now, Cæsar, let thy troops beset our gates, And bar each avenue; thy gath'ring fleets O'erspread the sea, and stop up ev'ry port; Cato shall open to himself a passage, And mock thy hopes.----

Por. Oh, sir! forgive your son, Whose grief hangs heavy on him. Oh, my father! How am I sure it is not the last time I e'er shall call you so? Be not displeased, Oh, be not angry with me whilst I weep, And, in the anguish of my heart, beseech you To quit the dreadful purpose of your soul!

Cato. Thou hast been ever good and dutiful.

[_Embracing him._]

Weep not, my son, all will be well again; The righteous gods, whom I have sought to please, Will succour Cato, and preserve his children.

Por. Your words give comfort to my drooping heart.

Cato. Portius, thou may'st rely upon my conduct: Thy father will not act what misbecomes him. But go, my son, and see if aught be wanting Among thy father's friends; see them embark'd, And tell me if the winds and seas befriend them. My soul is quite weigh'd down with care, and asks The soft refreshment of a moment's sleep.

Por. My thoughts are more at ease, my heart revives--

[_Exit_ CATO.]

[_Enter_ MARCIA.]

Oh, Marcia! Oh, my sister, still there's hope Our father will not cast away a life So needful to us all, and to his country. He is retired to rest, and seems to cherish Thoughts full of peace.--He has dispatch'd me hence With orders that bespeak a mind composed, And studious for the safety of his friends. Marcia, take care, that none disturb his slumbers.

[_Exit._]

Marcia. Oh, ye immortal powers, that guard the just, Watch round his couch, and soften his repose, Banish his sorrows, and becalm his soul With easy dreams; remember all his virtues, And show mankind that goodness is your care!

[_Enter_ LUCIA.]

Lucia. Where is your father, Marcia; where is Cato?

Marcia. Lucia, speak low, he is retired to rest. Lucia, I feel a gentle dawning hope Rise in my soul--We shall be happy still.

Lucia. Alas, I tremble when I think on Cato! In every view, in every thought, I tremble! Cato is stern and awful as a god; He knows not how to wink at human frailty, Or pardon weakness, that he never felt.

Marcia. Though stern and awful to the foes of Rome, He is all goodness, Lucia, always mild; Compassionate and gentle to his friends; Fill'd with domestic tenderness, the best, The kindest father; I have ever found him Easy and good, and bounteous to my wishes.

Lucia. 'Tis his consent alone can make us blest. Marcia, we both are equally involved In the same intricate,

perplex'd distress. The cruel hand of fate, that has
destroy'd Thy brother Marcus, whom we both lament----

Marcia. And ever shall lament; unhappy youth!

Lucia. Has set my soul at large, and now I stand
Loose of my vow. But who knows Cato's thoughts? Who
knows how yet he may dispose of Portius, Or how he has
determined of himself?

Marcia. Let him but live, commit the rest to Heav'n.

[_Enter_ LUCIUS.]

Luc. Sweet are the slumbers of the virtuous man! Oh,
Marcia, I have seen thy godlike father! Some power
invisible supports his soul, And bears it up in all its
wonted greatness. A kind, refreshing sleep is fall'n upon
him: I saw him stretch'd at ease; his fancy lost In pleasing
dreams; as I drew near his couch, He smiled, and cried,
"Cæsar, thou canst not hurt me."

Marcia. His mind still labours with some dreadful
thought.

[_Enter_ JUBA.]

Jub. Lucius, the horsemen are return'd from viewing
The number, strength, and posture of our foes, Who now
encamp within a short hour's march; On the high point
of yon bright western tower, We ken them from afar; the

setting sun Plays on their shining arms and burnish'd helmets, And covers all the field with gleams of fire.

Luc. Marcia, 'tis time we should awake thy father. Cæsar is still disposed to give us terms, And waits at distance, till he hears from Cato.

[_Enter_ PORTIUS.]

Portius, thy looks speak somewhat of importance, What tidings dost thou bring? Methinks, I see Unusual gladness sparkle in thy eyes.

Por. As I was hasting to the port, where now My father's friends, impatient for a passage, Accuse the ling'ring winds, a sail arrived From Pompey's son, who, through the realms of Spain, Calls out for vengeance on his father's death, And rouses the whole nation up to arms. Were Cato at their head, once more might Rome Assert her rights, and claim her liberty. But, hark! what means that groan?----Oh, give me way, And let me fly into my father's presence!

[_Exit._]

Luc. Cato, amidst his slumbers, thinks on Rome, And, in the wild disorder of his soul, Mourns o'er his country.--Ha! a second groan-- Heav'n guard us all!

Marcia. Alas, 'tis not the voice Of one who sleeps; 'tis agonizing pain-- 'Tis death is in that sound----

[_Enter_ PORTIUS.]

Por. Oh, sight of woe! Oh, Marcia, what we fear'd is
come to pass-- Cato has fall'n upon his sword----

Luc. Oh, Portius, Hide all the horrors of thy mournful
tale, And let me guess the rest.

Por. I've raised him up, And placed him in his chair;
where pale and faint, He gasps for breath, and, as his life
flows from him, Demands to see his friends. His servants
weeping, Obsequious to his order, bear him hither!----

Marcia. Oh, Heav'n! assist me in this dreadful hour, To
pay the last sad duties to my father!

[CATO _brought on, in a Chair._]

Cato. Here set me down---- Portius, come near
me--Are my friends embark'd? Can any thing be thought
of for their service? Whilst I yet live, let me not live
in vain---- Oh, Lucius, art thou here?--Thou art too
good-- Let this our friendship live between our children;
Make Portius happy in thy daughter Lucia---- Marcia,
my daughter---- Oh, bend me forward!----Juba loves thee,
Marcia-- A senator of Rome, while Rome survived, Would
not have match'd his daughter with a king-- But Cæsar's
arms have thrown down all distinction-- I'm sick to
death----Oh, when shall I get loose From this vain world,
th' abode of guilt and sorrow! And yet, methinks, a beam

of light breaks in On my departing soul----Alas, I fear
I've been too hasty!--Oh, ye powers, that search The heart
of man, and weigh his inmost thoughts, If I have done
amiss, impute it not---- The best may err, but you are
good, and--Oh!--

[_Dies._]

Por. There fled the greatest soul that ever warm'd
A Roman breast:-- From hence, let fierce contending
nations know, What dire effects from civil discord flow:
'Tis this that shakes our country with alarms; And gives
up Rome a prey to Roman arms; Produces fraud, and
cruelty, and strife, And robs the guilty world of Cato's
life.

[_Exeunt omnes._]

THE END.

PRINTED BY J. SMITH.

www.ingramcontent.com/pod-product-compliance
Lightning Source LLC
Chambersburg PA
CBHW060418310726
48976CB00003B/1097